WITHDRAWN

D0508367

Seaside Dances

The Seaside Hunters

by Stacy Claflin

http://www.stacyclaflin.com

Copyright ©2015 Stacy Claflin. All rights reserved.
Print Edition

Edited by Staci Troilo

This is a work of fiction. Any resemblance to actual persons living
or dead, businesses, events, or locales is purely coincidental or used
fictitiously. The author has taken great liberties with locales
including the creation of fictional towns.

Reproduction in whole or part of this publication without express
written consent is strictly prohibited. Do not upload or distribute
anywhere.

To receive book updates from the author, sign up here.
http://bit.ly/1ONrfMw

One

~

ZACHARY HUNTER NARROWED HIS DARK eyes, glaring at the punching bag as he sauntered toward it. He stood in front of it, balling up his bare fists. After all the stress—that he'd kept to himself—this was the ideal release.

He struck the bag. Even with the force of his pent-up frustration, he received little push-back.

Zachary pummeled it again. And then again. The skin on his knuckles hurt. He didn't care.

With each impact, he thought about everything that had gone wrong in New York.

The newspaper closing down. *Punch, punch.*

Those high and mighty publishers who refused to even look at his book. *Strike, strike.*

His agent, who hadn't worked hard enough for him. *Whomp, whomp.*

All the wasted time. *Bash.*

The wasted money. *Smash, smash.*

His failed relationship. *Punch, punch, punch.*

Now living with his parents. *Slam, slam.*

In his old bedroom. *Whack, whack, whack.*

It was all too much. Not all of it was his fault, but it didn't keep him from feeling like a massive failure.

This was not where he pictured his life at the cusp of thirty. *Bash. Bash.*

Jobless, without a book deal, recently dumped, and poor. *Strike, strike, strike.*

Zachary closed his eyes and continued his attack on the bag until sweat ran down his face and he felt warm liquid on his hands. Opening his eyes, he saw the blood. Great. Now he'd have to clean off the punching bag.

He glanced around the room, hoping no one in the gym was paying him any attention. He looked like a rookie, having forgotten to wrap his knuckles or put on gloves first. Luckily, everyone else was busy with their own workouts. There were no paper towels for cleaning the mess, so he would have to get some from the bathroom.

Covering his knuckles, he crossed the gym and went to his brother, Brayden, who jogged on a treadmill while reading a magazine.

"I gotta run out to the hall for a little bit," Zachary said.

Brayden wiped some sweat from his forehead with the towel resting on his shoulders. "Everything okay?"

Zachary stuffed his stinging hands into the pockets of his shorts. "Yeah. I'm just going to see if they added anything new to the club while I was in New York."

"I heard they added a ballet program," Brayden teased his younger brother.

"Thanks," Zachary muttered. He shook his head as he spun around and went into the hallway. He found the restrooms exactly where he remembered. He promptly washed the blood off his hands and then splashed cold water all over his face.

He stared at his reflection, almost startled at what he saw. It hadn't been so long ago that his features showed his once carefree spirit. Now he had a permanent frown, several days' worth of stubble, and dark bands under his eyes. Even his brown eyes seemed darker.

Zachary shook out his hands, trying to work out some of the pain. It had been a stupid idea to workout with his brother.

Brayden was a cardiologist, and as a result, was in perfect shape since heart health was always on his mind. Zachary, on the other hand, hadn't so much as looked at a gym in the last year. Probably longer. He sat at a desk writing all day, ignoring his muscles and added pounds.

Now his body ached from his head to toe. But, at the same time, his muscles felt good just from a little use. Maybe he *would* take up Brayden's offer to workout together a few times a week. He'd planned on backing out after this trial session. But it could be just what Zachary needed.

He grabbed a stack of paper towels for cleaning the punching bag, and went out into the hallway. As soon as he did, he ran right into someone.

"I'm sorry," Zachary said. "I wasn't looking."

"No, it was my fault." A pretty girl with brownish-red hair turned around and smiled at him.

He quickly hid his bruised hands behind his back. "Not at all."

Her bright eyes shone as her mouth continued to curve upward, as she held his gaze. "I wasn't paying attention. I'm heading to class."

"Ballet?" Zachary asked, noting her leotard. The style reminded him of the one Sophia, his late sister, had worn when she took dance lessons.

She nodded, pulling her long hair into a bun behind her head, securing it with a bright yellow band. "I'm teaching ballet to a bunch of silly girls."

A little girl in a tutu ran in between them, giggling.

"And that's one of them. Hey, Emma—slow down!"

"I will, Miss Jasmine!" the girl called. She spun around and crashed into another little girl in a tutu. Both girls fell to the floor and burst into tears as they landed.

Jasmine shook her head, sighing. "I'd better get going. Sorry again for crashing into you." She ran after the kids.

"It was my fault," Zachary called, but he doubted she'd heard him.

He watched Jasmine as she helped up the crying girls and got them laughing in a matter of moments. She dusted one off and spoke animatedly, keeping them in giggles.

Zachary admired her optimism. He'd once been like that. There was a time he would have wanted to have a girlfriend like her. But with his current state of mind, he would probably suck all her happiness away. Not that he even had time or the energy for another relationship. Especially after the way things had ended with Monica.

He remembered the blood on the punching bag, so he went back to the gym and wiped it off before anyone else needed the equipment.

Brayden walked his way, and Zachary threw the paper towels into the garbage, hoping his brother wouldn't notice.

"Are you done?" Zachary asked.

"Yeah," Brayden said. "I need to get to a meeting. So, did you decide? Want to make this a regular thing?"

Zachary paused. Did he really want to commit?

Brayden tilted his head, his eyes wide. "You know you want to."

"I was thinking about ballet," Zachary teased. He smiled, remembering his run-in with Jasmine. If he came regularly, he might see her again. Even though he didn't need distractions in his life, he couldn't help hoping to see her again.

Brayden gave him a playful hit on the arm. "Right. I

can just see you in a leotard."

"You'd rock it more than me," Zachary said, feeling a bit of his old self trying to come out.

Brayden laughed. "Anyway, I'll be back same time, same place in two days. Sound good?"

Zachary pretended to think about it. "Yeah, sure. I suppose I can do that." Maybe he could arrive a little early and see Jasmine again.

Brayden adjusted his gym bag over his shoulder. "Maybe next time we can try to catch up some more. I want to hear all about New York."

Zachary withheld a groan. "I'd rather hear more about your clinic. And Lana."

Brayden's face softened at the mention of his new fiancée. "Definitely. See you in a couple days."

"Sure. See you then," Zachary said. He went over to the lockers, grabbed his bag, and slung it over his shoulder. He glanced at the punching bag again, making sure he hadn't missed any blood. Once he was sure it was clean, he headed out to the hallway.

Zachary peered in all the windows along the way, curious about what other classes were in the club. He hadn't stepped foot in there since he was a teenager, competing with his friends to see who could lift the most weights. He turned down a corridor he didn't think had been there before.

In windows along the hallway, he could see all kinds of classes. Zumba, yoga, karate, kick-boxing, cross-training, swimming, and even tumbling toddlers. He couldn't remember the building being so big. They had to have added on at some point over the years.

He slowed down as he rounded a corner and found himself back near where he'd started. He passed more classes, but slowed at the last one. Jasmine was showing little girls how she spun on her toes.

All the little girls gathered around her with wide eyes. Some jumped up and down, and a few pushed each other to get closer to the front.

He kept walking, not wanting to be some creepy guy watching girls dance—not that it was the kids who held his interest. He slowed again, gazing back at Jasmine. She had stopped spinning, and now helped the young students get in their places.

Jasmine spun her arm around in front of her, and several of the children twirled around. One little girl had a difficult time with her balance, and Jasmine bent down to her level, holding one arm and leg so the girl could spin.

Zachary's heart warmed watching her, and a soft smile crept across his face. Having grown up as one of six siblings, he could appreciate anyone who had such patience with kids.

Footsteps sounded down the hall. Zachary straightened his back, readjusted the gym bag over his shoulder, and scrambled in the other direction.

When he got outside, he blinked fast to get his eyes

to adjust to the bright sunshine. Birds in a nearby tree sang as he breathed in the familiar ocean air. He had nowhere to be—since he was jobless and living with his parents—so he sat down on a bench not far from the building, soaking up the rays.

He sighed, enjoying the moment of relaxation. He hadn't taken any time for himself in a long time, and it felt even better after having worked out a little in the gym. The warm California sun massaged his sore muscles.

After a few minutes, he pulled out his Kindle from his bag and started reading. He loved the no-glare screen that allowed him to read anywhere. It was like having a book without having to lug his entire library around. He found the thriller he was reading—studying, actually—and opened it.

Despite his agent telling him how good his own manuscript was, Zachary couldn't help feeling like something was wrong with it. He had taken to purchasing every thriller novel he could find to compare to his own.

If it was so good, like his agent had told him countless times, then why wouldn't any of the publishers take a look at it? Big or small, none would touch it.

His stomach grew tight, so he rested his Kindle against his knee and groaned. Why couldn't he just focus on reading? No matter what he tried to focus on, his mind wandered back to the publishers and their refusal to even look at his work.

The agent had said it was one of the best she'd read in a long time. But she probably said that to all of her clients, or she was just a liar. Or maybe she just hadn't read many thrillers. Who knew? Certainly not him.

Sighing, Zachary went back to the novel he was reading and tried to figure out how it could get published when his couldn't. Zachary's dialog was better, and the action in this book sucked. Not that Zachary thought his debut novel was award-worthy, but it was definitely a good read. It was at least as good as half the ones out there.

He ran his fingers through his hair. There had to be a way he could convince someone influential to read it. Then it would get published for sure. The problem was finding someone while he was stuck in the small touristy town of Kittle Falls, all the way across the country from the big New York publishing houses.

Two

~

JASMINE BLACKWELL PUT THE BROOM away after sweeping the dance floor. Even though she didn't allow food in her classroom, crumbs always found their way onto her floor. She glanced over the room to make sure it was pristine for the next class. Everything seemed better than it had when she had come in. Not even a stray hair remained on the floor.

She walked over to the window to get her dance bag and her purse, but stopped when she saw who sat outside.

On a bench rested the hot guy who had bumped into her earlier in the hall. He was reading a tablet, but his face scrunched up like he didn't enjoy it. It was time to leave so she could punch her time card, but she wanted to keep watching him. There was something dark and mysterious about him.

Jasmine had hardly been able to look away from him after they had bumped into each other. He was gorgeous, despite being all sweaty. Maybe the sweat made him even more attractive, but either way, he was far better looking than anyone she'd seen in a long time. Even just sitting on the bench, unhappy, he was handsome.

Part of her wanted to go out there and strike up a conversation, but she had to get going. She was supposed to meet her roommate for dinner before hitting the nightly concert on the beach.

If she chose to chat up the hot guy, though, Kate would surely understand.

"Still here?" came a voice from behind.

Jasmine turned around, cheeks heating up. "I, uh, yeah. Just grabbing my stuff. How's it going, Olivia?"

"Oh, you know. Spent all day at the beach. I swear, this is the best internship ever."

Jasmine grabbed her bag and purse. "Yeah. I wasn't sold at first, but I have to say I love the town. See you at the concert tonight." She headed out the door, waving to the other dance instructor.

Jasmine went to the employee lounge and clocked her time card before leaving the building. Deciding to strike up a conversation with the alluring stranger, she took the long way around the building to where he'd been reading.

Disappointment ran through her when she saw some middle-aged guy sitting at the bench. He glanced up from his newspaper. "Into dance?" he asked.

"What?" Jasmine asked. If that was a strange pickup

line, she didn't want to stick around and find out. She hurried away, hoping she'd see that cute guy again.

Well, it was a small town. She was likely to run into him again, especially if he made a habit of going there to work out. She'd just have to make a special effort to keep a lookout for him—and find an excuse to get his number.

Jasmine's phone buzzed, letting her know she had a text. She glanced at it, knowing it was probably her roommate. Sure enough, Kate was already at the restaurant wondering where she was.

Jasmine sent her a quick message. *Almost there.*

She picked up her pace and jogged down the walkway until she reached the cute diner they'd agreed on. It was a bit early for dinner, but at least they'd beat the rush. Once five o'clock hit, every restaurant in town filled up.

Kate and Jasmine had a full kitchen in their rental condo, but it was so much easier to just eat out. It didn't involve cooking or cleaning up. It made their internship feel more like a vacation than work.

She hadn't been excited at first. Not by a long shot. Kittle Falls had actually been her last choice of places to intern. Her eyes had been set on a couple large dance companies in Portland, but they had filled up quickly.

With Kittle Falls being a touristy beach town, the classes she taught changed kids nearly every week as families came and went. In Portland, she would have been able to teach the same kids all summer, watching them learn, grow, and blossom as young dancers. Now she had to start fresh every week most of the time.

Sometimes kids stayed around for a couple weeks. There were actually a few staying the whole summer, and even one girl who lived in town, but Jasmine had to start from scratch every Monday because of all the new dancers in her class each week.

If nothing else, Jasmine would become great at dealing with new kids. She still got some practice with the few who remained every week, so she at least got *some* experience helping them become experienced dancers.

"What took you so long?" Kate asked when Jasmine sat down at the table. She was already eating an appetizer.

Jasmine stole a jalapeno popper from the basket. "Took me a little longer to clean up today," she fibbed, not wanting to admit to being distracted by a cute guy.

"Someone pee on the floor again?" Kate asked.

"Please. We're eating."

"I'm eating. You're late." Kate stuck a fried cheese stick in her mouth.

"You're sharing." Jasmine took an onion ring and ate that. "And I'm starving."

"Did you see the dancing pigs at the beach earlier?" Kate asked, rolling her eyes.

"Must have missed that." Jasmine was glad she'd spent her time watching the mystery man rather than dancing swine.

"They have the craziest stuff around here," Kate said. "I can't believe you wanted to stick around Portland. Boring."

"And I can't believe this was your first choice," Jasmine said. "Where's the challenge?"

Kate's eyes widened. "Beach. Town."

"Sorry. Guess I was more concerned with my career."

"It's an internship," Kate said, "and it's not like we studied dance at Julliard."

"Still, I'm serious about my career." Jasmine took a sip of water.

Kate raised an eyebrow. "And that's why you're eating out all summer? To keep your figure for the job?"

"I eat healthy breakfasts and lunches."

Kate didn't look convinced. "That's true, I guess. You've filled our fridge with fruits and veggies. Does that counteract all this grease?"

"Seems to work." Jasmine shrugged.

The waitress came over, and they gave her the order for dinner.

"We need to meet some guys," Kate said. "No offense. I like hanging out with you and everything, but we're acting like old ladies, eating by ourselves all the time."

"Aside from the concerts, I don't have much time," Jasmine said. "I've got the classes, and when they're not in session, I'm busy with the lesson plans."

"Seriously?" Kate asked. "We get new kids every week. Just do the same one over and over. It's not like the kids know the difference. Easy-peasy."

"The kids who come every week don't want to do the same routine all the time," Jasmine said.

"Yeah, but there's only one or two. They don't care."

"Sure they do," Jasmine insisted. "They'll get bored. Even if they don't say anything."

Kate stuffed some fries in her mouth.

Jasmine shook her head.

Kate smiled. "I haven't had any complaints."

"I want the returning girls to walk away with real skills," Jasmine said. "I want to make a difference."

"It's dancing, not the Peace Corps."

Jasmine sighed. It was pointless to argue with Kate. The two of them were polar opposites, but somehow that made their friendship stronger. Kate helped Jasmine to be a bit more spontaneous, and Jasmine helped to keep Kate focused.

"So, where do you plan on finding a guy?" Jasmine asked.

Kate's eyes lit up. "I thought about the beach, but it seems like everyone's always either paired off or otherwise busy."

"Jump in on a game of volleyball or something," Jasmine said.

"And break a nail?" Kate asked. "No thanks."

"You know what I mean. Something. You're athletic."

"There is this one guy at the club." Kate grinned, looking deep in thought.

Jasmine's heart raced. She hoped it wasn't the same guy she'd been staring at through the window. "Oh?" she asked weakly.

"Yeah, he's from England or somewhere. I could listen to him talk all day, even if it was about politics. You should hear him speak—you'd melt into a puddle. Oh, that accent." Kate sighed dramatically.

Relief swept through Jasmine. "Why don't you ask him out?"

"I should, huh?" Kate asked, sitting taller.

The waitress brought their food, and they dug in.

"Salad?" Kate asked. "Really? I thought dinner was for grease."

"Didn't you hear me order?" Jasmine asked.

Kate shrugged, dipping a fry into her shake and then sticking it in her mouth.

"I need to break the habit." The summer was winding down, and she didn't want to be used to fast food every night when she returned to Oregon.

"Maybe I should eat better, too." Kate sighed. "I wouldn't have to workout so hard to burn calories."

"Precisely." Jasmine bit into a piece of kale covered in almonds, cranberries, and a light sauce.

"Don't you get hungry all the time?" Kate asked, not appearing convinced.

"No. Just snack on healthy stuff throughout the day. Oh, and drink plenty of water."

Kate's eyes glazed over. "Did you watch *Dance America* last night?" she asked, obviously changing the subject. "They eliminated Luciano. I about died—I thought for sure he would win."

"I was already in bed." Between the internship and nightly beach concerts, Jasmine couldn't stay awake for television.

"Of course," Kate said. She went on about how much she adored Luciano and what a talented dancer he was.

"Maybe he needs a girlfriend," Jasmine said.

Kate snorted. "Yeah, right. I think I'll stick to some guys in the area who I actually have a shot with."

They made light conversation and finished their meal, leaving just as the restaurant filled up with the nightly crowd. They had to squeeze past a group of people standing near the door, waiting to be seated.

"The concert doesn't start for another hour and a half," Jasmine said. "What do you want to do?"

"Go back to the condo and change." Kate stared at her.

Jasmine looked down. "Oh, I totally forgot to put on my regular clothes."

Kate laughed. "Yeah, you've been in your leotard

this whole time."

Jasmine's face flushed with heat. She'd been so distracted by watching that guy she'd forgotten to change.

Kate gave her a funny expression, but didn't say anything.

Jasmine was grateful because she didn't want to talk about the mystery man. For all she knew, he already had a girlfriend or maybe she'd never see him again. With so many people coming and going through town, that was real possibility.

They made their way to the condo, Kate still talking about Luciano being cut from the reality show. When they got inside, Jasmine ran to the bathroom to get cleaned up and change her clothes. Her mind kept wandering back to the cute guy. It wasn't like her to obsess over a man, but there was something about him that she just couldn't shake.

She was conflicted. On one hand, she wanted to get to know him. On the other, she needed to spend the rest of her summer focusing on the internship. If she received a stellar recommendation, that would help her get the job of her dreams. She hadn't managed to intern at either of the studios she wanted, but that didn't mean she couldn't work at one once she had the proper training.

Jasmine decided to push him out of her mind and leave it up to chance. If she saw him again, then it would be her sign to at least talk with him. If she didn't, then it wasn't meant to be.

In the meantime, she had to keep her head clear, and he wasn't helping, whatever his name was.

When she got out of the bathroom, Kate was ready to go. She had on cutoff shorts over a brightly-colored one piece swimsuit. Jasmine felt overdressed for the beach in a skirt and short-sleeved shirt, but she wasn't about to change.

"Ready?" asked Kate.

"Let's go." Jasmine grabbed her purse and they headed back to the beach. Music reached them long before they hit the sand.

"I hear the band—they're already warming up," Kate squealed. "They sound good, don't you think?"

"Definitely." Jasmine glanced over to where people were already crowded around the stage.

Kate ran ahead of her, and Jasmine was forced to run also, or she would lose Kate and never find her again—not during the concert anyway.

A headache started to form. It was going to be a long night, and she didn't feel much like being smashed up against a bunch of strangers.

Three

❧

ZACHARY ROLLED OVER IN BED, every movement hurting more than the last. Muscles he didn't know existed ached. He groaned, not wanting to get up. Next time, he would remember to warm up. That's what he got for going more than a year without working out.

His mom called his name from the other side of his door.

"I'll get up," he called, rubbing his right arm. Not that getting out of bed mattered. He had no plans for the day, so his parents would be the only ones who knew or cared if he did nothing.

"When?" asked his mom, her voice muffled through the door.

"Soon!" He stretched his legs. His right leg throbbed with intense pain as he got a charley horse.

"Breakfast is ready," she called.

Zachary bit his lip, stretching his leg to work out the muscle spasm.

"Did you hear me?"

He picked up a book from his nightstand and threw it at his door. That should answer the question.

"I'll take that as yes." The floor in the hall creaked as she walked away. He could hear her complaining about her moodiest son.

Zachary grabbed his leg and rubbed the pained muscle. Next time he would definitely stretch more before working out.

Finally, after what felt like forever, the pain subsided and he was able to breathe normally again. He rolled over again and sat up, ignoring each and every muscle that screamed in protest.

This was going to be a long day, and he hoped his parents would spend most of it at the Hunter Family Store. With the summer winding down, they were likely to be extra busy before everything calmed down for the rest of the year.

Zachary stood, his legs hurting all the more. He reached down to pick up a shirt from the floor and nearly pulled a muscle in his chest. He stopped and stood back up, taking deep breaths.

That was better. His family could live with seeing him shirt-free. It wasn't worth the struggle.

He walked into the hall, moving like a robot. He went into the bathroom. The mirror showed the start of a beard, but he didn't care. He had no desire to shave today. Or do anything other than take a long, hot shower to hopefully soothe his muscles.

Someone knocked on the door. "Your mom made breakfast," said his dad.

"I need a shower first."

"She made your favorite, and if it gets cold, you'll hurt her feelings."

Zachary groaned. Some things never changed, and he knew better than to let the meal chill.

"Be right there." He splashed cold water on his face and ran a comb through his hair. He made his way to the kitchen, taking ten times longer than it should have due to his aching muscles.

His parents sat with Cruz, eating omelets and bacon. Cruz wore a shirt with the sleeves ripped off, showing off his numerous tattoos.

"Look who's up," Cruz said. "You gonna help me out at the shop today, yo?"

"Not today," Zachary said. He grimaced at a sore muscle.

"Why?" asked Cruz. "Got important plans?"

"Please put a shirt on," his mom said. "My kitchen, my rules. You need to wear clothes at the table."

"I am wearing clothes."

She looked him over, looking concerned. "What's wrong?" She stared at his beaten-up hands.

He stuffed them in his shorts pocket. "Just a little sore today, that's all. It's no big deal."

"Oh, did you finally work out with Brayden?" asked his dad.

"Yeah," Zachary said. "It's been a while, and now I'm feeling it."

"Well, your mom's right. Put on a shirt."

"He just wants to show off how ripped he is," Cruz joked.

"Shut up," Zachary muttered, glaring at his younger brother.

"Dude, I was just messin' with you. You don't even look like you stopped working out."

"Whatever." Zachary turned around and started the slow trek back to his room.

Halfway down the hall, Cruz joined him. "Are you really that sore, man? Lemme just get your shirt for you. Stay there." Cruz ran to Zachary's room and came out a minute later with a dark blue shirt Zachary didn't recognize. "It was all I could find. Sorry."

He tossed it at him. Zachary held it up and saw that it was an old t-shirt from high school—and even worse, it had the *Superman* logo across the chest. It was hardly the only shirt Cruz could have found. He'd had to have dug to the back of Zachary's closet to find this relic.

Sighing, Zachary slid it on. It clung to him so tightly that it was no better than being shirtless.

When he walked into the kitchen, his brother burst out laughing. "I wish I hadn't left my phone at the shop last night. Someone has to get a picture."

"No. Someone better not." Zachary glared at Cruz.

Their mom shook her head at the two of them. "Do

boys ever grow up?"

Zachary was too sore to think up a funny comeback. He robot-walked to the table and picked up a piece of bacon, shoving it into his mouth. It melted on his tongue.

Cruz burst out laughing.

"What's so funny?" asked Zachary.

"I just love your shirt, Zach. You should wear that to the beach today, *Superman*."

"It's Zachary. Not Zach—and certainly not *Superman*."

"You should get to the shop, Cruz," said their dad. "It's almost opening time."

Cruz wiped a tear from his eye. "Calvin's got it this morning. He can hold the fort until I get there. Can you at least leave the shirt on until I get back for lunch?" He grinned at Zachary.

"If you like *Superman* so much, you should get a tattoo," Zachary said.

Cruz laughed. "I thought you were going to tell me to marry him."

"That, too."

Their dad shook his head, but it was obvious he was trying not to laugh.

Zachary ignored his family and dug into the omelet. His parents discussed the family business until Cruz finally left for work.

His mom turned to Zachary. "When are you going

to get a job?" asked his mom.

"I just got back. I need to figure some things out first."

"It's been almost three weeks," his dad said. "And you spent a week on the road driving from New York to California."

"My agent thinks I need to write another book," Zachary said, "and if I do that, I can't have a job tying me down."

His dad poured some orange juice. "You managed to work at the paper when you were in New York."

Zachary took a deep breath and counted to ten silently. "I wasn't writing a novel then. My agent already had it, and she chased every publishing company, no matter how big or small, while I chased stories for the column."

"Well, you need to do something. Lying around in your room all day isn't getting you anywhere."

"I'll start outlining my next novel today. Does that work?" Zachary asked.

"What's wrong with the first book?" asked his mom. "You said the agent liked it."

"Yeah, she does, but it doesn't do any good if no one will look at it. She thinks I need something with a little romance. Right now that's what they're looking for in their thrillers." He shrugged. "Doesn't make sense to me, but that's what they demand."

"Can't you just add some into the story you already

wrote?" asked his dad.

Zachary shook his head. "No. It would be too contrived. I'll wait until they're ready for this one. In the next year or two, they won't want romance in thrillers anymore."

"Maybe you should get a girlfriend," his mom said. "That might inspire you to think romantically."

Zachary stood up, pushing his chair back. "I have plenty of things to draw from, thank you." He tried storming out of the kitchen, but his muscles wouldn't cooperate, and he moved with the grace of a giant marshmallow. He could hear his parents chuckling.

Maybe a job wasn't such a bad idea. Then he could get his parents off his back. Of course he didn't want to be a freeloader, but he did need a little time to get back on his feet.

As soon as he reached the bathroom, he gladly pulled off the old shirt. He got into the shower, getting the water as hot as his skin would allow. His muscles relaxed, and hopefully enough so that he would be able to move around like a human again before long.

When the water went cold, he got out and went to his room to find clothes that actually fit. After getting dressed, he went through his closet and drawers, taking out all the clothes from his childhood. No more tight-fitting, goofy superhero shirts for him.

He went out to the garage and found some empty plastic boxes and brought them into his room, packing away old memories. He stopped when he got to a shirt that Sophia, his sister, had given him before she'd gotten sick. He couldn't bring himself to put it away, so he folded it and put it in the back of his shirt drawer. He probably wouldn't wear again—he didn't want to risk anything happening to it—but he also didn't want to pack it up.

A lump formed in his throat thinking about her. That seemed to happen a lot still. It had been a few years, but he still felt as raw over losing his baby sister as when it happened. He tried to not to think about it— her passing—but usually tried to focus on her life. She'd had such a bright, beautiful smile and could always cheer anyone up.

He could sure use some of her enthusiasm now. Zachary could almost hear her telling him to keep trying. She'd always believed that he would one day get the publishing deal of his dreams. He sat on the bed, not feeling any better after the imaginary pep talk.

Being a creative type, Zachary was prone to a lot of different moods. It wasn't unusual for something others considered small to set him off, either angering him or hurting his feelings, but he rarely admitted to the latter. Sometimes he would fall into a mild depression and not even know why.

Growing up, his brothers had teased him, saying he was as emotional as any girl. He knew it wasn't true, and especially after hanging out with other creatives, he knew it was just the territory of being imaginative.

Sophia had always seemed to understand that, being a bit of a creative herself. Though she didn't usually do much with it, she was a fantastic artist. She claimed that it bored her, but she'd been the one who understood him more than any of the other Hunters.

Zachary held up the shirt again, thinking of something else he could do with it besides stuff it in a drawer. He'd seen frames for shirts—perhaps he could get one of those. Or maybe he could do something even more creative like have it made into a pillow or something like that. Sophia would have liked that.

He blinked back some tears, cleared his throat, and finished boxing up the rest of his old stuff. Sure, this was his childhood room, but that didn't mean it had to stay that way. He had everything from his tiny apartment that he could fit into his car, and he could make this room every bit as cool as his old place had been.

Zachary bent over to pick up one of the boxes and quickly remembered how sore he was. This was not going to hold him back anymore today. He needed some painkillers—why hadn't he thought of that sooner? It could have spared him the humiliation of wearing that too-tight shirt. Thankfully, Cruz hadn't had his phone to snap a picture.

He went out to the bathroom to search through the medicine cabinet. There was a bottle of aspirin that he swore had been there since he was in school. Checking the date, he saw he wasn't far off.

Zachary threw the bottle in the trash and kept looking until he found some ibuprofen that was only a couple years expired. He made a mental note to buy something new the next time he went to the shop. Didn't anyone else have aches and pains around here?

His mom walked by and peeked in. "What happened here?" she asked, looking at the counter now filled with the contents of the cabinet.

"I don't think anyone has gone through here in years. I threw out a bottle of medicine that was ten years old."

"Really? Thanks for doing that, Zach. I hate throwing anything away that belongs to any of you kids."

"None of us are kids anymore."

She sighed. "Don't remind me."

"Just think," he said, "soon enough, kids will be running around again."

Her face lit up. "I'm so excited about Jake and Tiffany's baby. Who would've ever thought he'd be the first of you boys to become a dad?"

"That just sounds weird. I can't imagine him a parent."

"You'll be an uncle. Uncle Zach. It has a nice ring to it."

"Yes, Uncle Zachary sure does."

Four

~

JASMINE COULD HARDLY PAY ATTENTION to the class she was teaching. Luckily, it was a simple routine, similar to many others she'd taught. She kept hoping the cute guy would come back to the gym. So far, she hadn't seen him, though she jumped every time someone walked by the window.

"What's up?" asked Brooke, one of the girls.

This class was jazz for teens, and those girls didn't miss anything. The kiddie ballet had gone along as usual as Jasmine sneaked peeks.

"Oh, I thought I saw someone," Jasmine said. "It's no big deal."

"Seems like it is," Brooke said. "You're paying more attention to the window than us." She raised an eyebrow.

Jasmine stretched her arm. "You just volunteered yourself to show the class the routine we just went over."

"What?" Brooke whined. "No."

The other girls egged her on until Brooke came to

the front of the class, scowling at Jasmine.

"You'll do great," Jasmine said, leaning against a wall where she could both look out the window *and* watch the girls without being too obvious.

After Brooke went back to her spot, no one else said anything about Jasmine looking out the window constantly. She noticed some of the girls watching her, but no one said a word.

When the jazz class was over, she had a two hour break before a couple kiddie classes. Jasmine changed out of her dance clothes and into shorts and a tank top. Stomach rumbling, she headed back for her classroom.

She'd made herself a sack lunch for the day and she ate it in her class, keeping her eyes out for him from both windows—the club hallway and the outside benches. Assuming he came by her classroom again, she wouldn't miss him.

She checked the time. He'd come later the day before, so she was probably being too jumpy expecting him before the mid-afternoon. Part of her was embarrassed by her obsession over the guy who she'd only spoken a few words to—that's why she wouldn't even tell Kate about him. At least not yet.

If she at least got his name, then maybe she could bring him up to her. Kate might tease her, but they could also have a lot of fun with a double date. Kate was obsessed with meeting guys. She saw this summer as a final hurrah before entering the real world as a dance instructor.

Actually, that was the mindset of a lot of the other interns. It seemed that most of them had decided to come to Kittle Falls because it was a fun beach town, not because they were going to have an exciting internship.

Jasmine took the last bite of her banana and aimed the peel at the garbage, making a basket. She turned to back to her spot by the window and nearly choked. He was back at the benches outside! She scrambled to put all of her food away, and then she grabbed her purse and ran into the hall, taking the shortest route to where he sat.

When she opened the door, she straightened up and pretended she was only wandering out for no other reason than to get some sun. He didn't even look up when the loud door slammed behind her. Once again, he was lost in his tablet, but at least he was still there.

Her mind raced trying to figure out a good way to start the conversation. The weather? No. It was always, always sunny here. She could ask about his tablet, but that might be too nosy, especially since he looked so upset over it before.

Jasmine wanted to smack herself. When was she ever one to be shy? She spoke easily with nearly everyone. The only people she didn't like talking to were self-centered jerks. The hot, built guy in front of her wasn't one. That much was clear from their short conversation the day before.

She forced one foot in front of the other until she stood in front of the bench where he sat. He still didn't look up so she sat on the other end and inched closer, seeing if she could pull his attention away from the device.

He didn't budge, so she cleared her throat.

Finally, he looked up. He appeared confused, but then his face lit up. "Jasmine. Sorry, I didn't recognize you without her leotard."

Butterflies danced in her stomach. He remembered her name? She smiled. "No problem. I don't think I caught your name." She held out her hand.

He grasped it and shook. He had nice firm grip and she caught a whiff of his cologne. It smelled like sandalwood. "I'm Zachary. Sorry again about bumping into you."

Jasmine laughed. "Oh, it's no problem. Now it looks like I've bumped into you."

He nodded. "Looks like it."

They stared at each other and Jasmine's mind raced for something to say. "So, what brings you to Kittle Falls?"

"I grew up here."

She waited for him to say more, but he didn't. It wasn't really a surprise that the mysterious guy was the silent type. Shy, maybe?

"Really?" Jasmine asked. "I haven't met many locals,

and your accent sounds different."

"I spent some time in New York," he said, "and I suppose it wore off on me."

"Maybe that's it," she said. "What were you doing there?"

Zachary looked uncomfortable. "I was working at a newspaper, but it shut down."

"Yeah?" she asked. "I've seen a lot of that in Portland."

He nodded again, squirming in his seat. "Is that where you're from?"

She bit her lip. That was a loaded question. "I am," she said, opting to keep it simple. "This summer is just for an internship."

"Dancing?" he asked, finally sounding a little engaged.

Jasmine's pulse raced. She loved talking about dance. "I'm working to be a dance instructor. I spent some time traveling and being in various programs around the country, but now I'm ready to settle down in one place for a bit."

"What kind of programs?" he asked.

"Probably the only one you would've heard of is the Nutcracker."

"I have. Isn't that a prestigious one to get into?" he asked, looking impressed.

"It is, because everyone who's anyone has heard of it. People clamor for tickets at Christmastime."

"I'm glad I've heard of it. That makes me someone." He smiled—and what a smile. It lit up his whole face.

Now might be the time to get his number. She took a deep breath. "So, Zach, do you—"

"Zachary," he corrected.

Jasmine stared at him, flustered. "I'm sorry." What was she going to ask him?

He shrugged.

"So, do you come by the gym much?" she asked.

He squirmed again, the smile fading. "I plan to. I haven't been back to town long, but my brother and I are going to make it a regular thing."

Good. That meant she would probably see him again. She tried to think of something interesting to say, but her mind was racing.

He glanced down at his Kindle like he wanted to get back to reading.

"Well, it's nice to keep bumping into you." She smiled.

"Um, yeah. You, too." He seemed nervous, and it was adorable.

But Jasmine didn't know why she made him feel that way. She'd never thought of herself as someone intimidating. "My roommate and I are planning on going to the concert on the beach tonight. Maybe we can bump into each other again there."

"I'm not really one for those crowds." Zachary glanced back down at his reader.

She looked him over, trying to figure him out. He was tall, buff, and so gorgeous... and it was multiplied by a thousand when he smiled. But at the same time, he was nowhere near as arrogant as he could be. In fact, he seemed a little bit—or maybe more than a little— awkward. A nerdy hot guy?

He looked away, playing with a strap on his tablet's case.

"We could always bump into each other somewhere else, you know," Jasmine said, realizing she was going to have to be the bold one. "Everyone has to eat. Want to run into each other at a restaurant?"

Zachary looked at her, surprised. "You want to go out with me?"

Jasmine's heart raced. She hadn't expected him to be so forward with his question. "Actually, I would. How does dinner sound?"

"Tonight?"

She couldn't help smiling. "Yeah. Unless you have other plans."

He looked deep in thought. "Nope. Not tonight."

Jasmine's smile widened. "Do you have a favorite place to eat?"

"To tell you the truth," he said, "I'm not even sure what's around here anymore. A lot has changed over the last few years."

Jasmine nodded. "There's a cute little diner near the beach. It's usually not too loud."

"That sounds perfect. What time?"

They discussed the details, and then he said he had to go help his brother with something.

"Can I get your number?" she asked, finally remembering what she was going to ask him before.

"Oh, right. That would be helpful, wouldn't it?" He looked flustered, and it was the cutest thing she'd seen.

"What's your number?" she asked, pulling out her phone.

He told her, and then she punched it in her phone and called him. "Now you have mine, too."

Zachary flashed his gorgeous smile. "See you at five."

"At five." Zachary got up and walked away, reading his tablet as he went.

Jasmine smiled, shaking her head. It was hard to know what to make of him, but at least she finally had a name—and a date. Whenever she'd met anyone who looked as good as him, they strutted around, fully aware of how good looking they were.

Not Zachary. There was something both mysterious and geeky about him, and now that Jasmine had a date lined up, she was even more curious about him than before. Was he just shy? An awkward, bookworm type? Maybe a brooding, deep thinker?

It would take some work to bring him out of his shell. She liked the idea of the challenge. He seemed like a wonderful person deep down, and if nothing else, she would at least enjoy the scenery as she fought to find out.

Jasmine leaned against the bench and took in the sun's warm rays. She closed her eyes, picturing Zachary in her mind, holding onto the image of his smile. She couldn't describe what that did to her—beyond melting her insides—but couldn't wait to meet him at the diner that night.

Her phone rang and she picked it up, not bothering to open her eyes and see who it was.

"Jasmine," said Kate, "Where are you?"

She sat upright, opening her eyes. "Did I miss an appointment? I—"

"No. It's just that usually you show up at the beach during your lunch break."

"Oh, sorry. There's this guy I met, and—"

"You met a guy?" Kate asked, her voice exaggerated. "Tell me everything."

"There isn't much to tell… yet. He's the quiet, mysterious type."

"Is he sexy?" Kate asked, sounding desperate for information.

"He's really good looking, and we're meeting for dinner tonight."

"Oh," Kate said. "This is good news. When do I get to meet him? I know, bring him to the concert tonight."

"He's not really into those."

"Bummer. Where are you going for dinner? I want

to get a peek."

Jasmine laughed. "He's mine, though."

"I wouldn't try to cut in on you. I'm so excited you finally took your eyes off your classes and met a guy." Kate almost sounded more excited than Jasmine. Almost. "What does he look like?"

"He's tall and muscular with dark brownish-green eyes. And he seems like he's… studious, maybe. He's mysterious."

"Nice. Short hair, long hair?" asked Kate.

"I don't know. Average?"

"But you said he's hot?"

Jasmine sighed. "So much. And that smile…oh, it's to die for."

"Can't wait to meet him. So, do you have time to hang out?" Kate asked.

Jasmine pulled her phone away, looking at the time on the screen. "Not today. I have to get back to my classroom and get everything set up for the next class pretty soon. By the time I got to the beach, I'd just have to turn around and leave."

"You met a guy," Kate said. "Better excuse than any. Can't wait to meet him."

And Jasmine couldn't wait to see him again.

Five

~

ZACHARY TOOK ANOTHER EXPIRED PAINKILLER as he brushed his hair, unhappy with how he looked. His hair had always given him trouble, but it seemed to act up even worse when he wanted to look good.

He didn't know what Jasmine had seen in him—she certainly hadn't caught him on his best day. Sore and tired from the day before, and still trying to get over all the junk from New York.

The last thing he needed was another relationship. It had nearly been two months since Monica had walked away from him—and told him every reason he sucked as not only a boyfriend, but as a human, too. He knew she was just being cruel.

It still hurt, though. And he still wondered if some of it were true. Maybe more than he thought.

They had been a bad match from the beginning, but somehow ended up dating for over a year, nearly destroying each other in the process. She'd learned quickly that though he was quiet, Zachary was strong and wouldn't be manipulated. Quiet didn't mean pushover, and he wasn't about to be intimidated by her name-calling or temper.

Her thing had always been to say hateful things to try to open him up. She said that at least when he was angry he spoke his mind. Sure, Zachary was quieter than most, but putting him down had been a horrible way to try to draw him out. Calling him names only made him want to shut Monica out all the more.

It had turned into a nasty vicious cycle of him keeping everything in and of her taunting him more. Then one day she attacked him verbally after he'd found out that the paper was closing—and he would be the first to go. That had been the day he finally told Monica what he thought of her communication style. She wanted to know what he thought? She got it—in full, living color.

Monica turned around and told him what a stuck-up, insecure jerk he was—only using much more vivid words—and to top it all off, she told him it was over, and she wanted nothing to do with him ever again. She'd told him what he could do to himself with his laptop and tablet, and she stormed out of his life.

Zachary was glad he'd never let her move in like she'd wanted so badly. That was another thing that caused a lot of conflict. He'd been brought up to be a gentleman, but she didn't want one. Monica had wanted a wild partier. Something he clearly was not.

Even though Zachary knew the breakup wasn't a

reflection on him, he couldn't help reeling from it. And when the money stopped coming in, all the horrible things she'd said about him ran circles through his head.

He had to get away from the East Coast and the rejection—both from Monica and the publishing houses. A man could only take so much, and he'd had all he could take. Coming back home and focusing on his next novel seemed like the perfect option. He could write without being distracted by a pointless job or a soul-sucking relationship.

Sure, he knew he'd have to deal with his parents bugging him about his writing, but as long as actively wrote, he knew they would be supportive. He didn't want to be a bum anymore than they wanted to support one. Zachary just needed a few more weeks to pull himself together.

He knew he was better than anyone in New York realized, and soon he would believe it again. Maybe this date with Jasmine would help. She seemed to like him despite his nervousness when she approached him earlier.

So many things had run through his mind that he had a hard time getting his mouth to cooperate. He was surprised she even wanted to get to know him after talking with him for those brief minutes.

He certainly hadn't been the best conversationalist. With every word she said to him, twenty negative thoughts filled his mind, either spoken by Monica or some heartless publishing house who wouldn't even read the opening of his book.

Zachary looked in the mirror and forced a grin. Brayden had always told him that it was his smile that made all the girls melt. It was decent, but he wasn't sure it had that kind of power.

Shrugging, he finally left the bathroom.

"You look nice," his mom said as he passed the living room.

"Are you going somewhere?" asked his dad.

Zachary considered not telling them, and then decided to. "I think I have a date."

"You *think?*" his dad asked.

Zachary sighed. "I'm meeting a girl for dinner. I guess that qualifies."

His mom's face lit up. "I'm so glad to see you coming out of your shell. Have fun."

"See you guys later." Zachary checked the time. He was running a little late, so he would have to drive rather than walk. Parking wasn't the greatest in the touristy areas, but maybe he'd find something close. And hopefully Jasmine wouldn't see the car. His little junker was embarrassing. He'd had to trade down in order to afford living in New York.

Everyone tried to convince him to lose the car completely because it was such a pain to drive around the city, but he wanted it in case he needed out. If he hadn't had the car, he would've had to borrow money from his parents to return home, and he wouldn't have done that.

Zachary drove to the diner and parked a block away, hoping Jasmine wouldn't see him getting in or out. When he got inside, he saw her already waiting in a booth.

"Sorry," he said, sitting across from her. "I meant to be on time."

"Do you always apologize so much?" She smiled sweetly. "This is the third time we've talked, and the third time you've started off with an apology."

He almost apologized, but stopped himself. "Too polite for my own good."

Jasmine's eyes sparkled. "No worries. I don't mind you bumping into me, and I don't mind you being five minutes late. I was nearly late myself." She shrugged. "I ordered us an appetizer. I hope that's okay."

"Sounds good." He smiled, feeling at ease in her presence.

"No tablet?" she asked, her tone teasing. But her face showed no cruelty—she had the face of an angel.

"Not on a date." Zachary's heart pummeled to the floor. "Uh, this is a date, right?" Zachary wanted to climb under the table and hide. He didn't talk much, but when he did, his mouth always seemed to mess something up. That's why he preferred writing. The delete button was a lifesaver.

"I sure hope so." The corners of her mouth twitched

upward.

They stared into each other's eyes. Jasmine's were a bright brown, unlike any he'd seen before. They were really pretty, much like her. "So, uh, how were the rest of your classes?" he asked, feeling a bit awkward with the silence.

Her face lit up. "Always interesting. You never know what you'll get when kids are involved." She laughed. "Today a girl fell over and knocked over another girl and then it turned into a domino effect, and half the class went down. Some of the kids were laughing, but a few were pretty mad. I wasn't sure whether to laugh or cry, but once I got everyone back up, they were all happy again."

Zachary found himself relaxing, and he laughed along with Jasmine. "Sounds like quite an adventure."

"It usually is." Her eyes shone as she continued smiling. "How about your work?"

He considered his wording. "There's a lot of action, too."

She looked curious. "How so?"

His heart pounded. Zachary hated talking about his writing in general, but especially now, with so much rejection tied to it. "I'm writing a novel."

Jasmine's eyes lit up. "Really? That's so cool. What's it about?"

It took him a moment to realize what she'd asked. Monica had never asked about his book—she'd always told him how he should write it, never once listening to his ideas. He swallowed. "It's a thriller."

"About…?" Jasmine stared into his eyes, appearing eager to hear more.

Zachary cleared his throat, his pulse racing. "The main character is trying to find the man who killed his dad. He finds him, but the assassin is deep within the Russian mafia, and Damion has to figure out how to gain their trust. But in the process, he gets intrigued and loses his focus." He paused. "I'm not describing it very well. That doesn't sound very thrilling." Maybe that was part of the reason he couldn't get anyone to give the book a chance—he needed to find a way to make it sound as exciting as it actually was.

"No," Jasmine said, "it sounds really good. Can I read it?"

"What?" Zachary asked, unsure he'd heard her right.

"I love a good book that will keep me up at night."

"It's not published or anything. It's a real work in progress, needing to be edited and—"

"I couldn't place a comma in the right place to save my life, anyway. I don't care about that. I'd love to read your story. It sounds great."

Zachary's face heated up. "I'm not sure."

"Why?" she asked. "Please? I'd love to read a book before it's released to the world. It would be an honor." She begged him with her beautiful eyes.

An honor? How could he say no to that?

"Okay." He couldn't believe he was going to let her read his book. He barely knew her. "I'll have to email it to you. You know how to side-load files?"

"I can look it up." She pulled out her phone. "I'll text you my email address."

Zachary's heart continued to race. No one other than his agent had actually read it. Sure, they'd sent it out to every publishing house, but no one had taken the time to get past the query letter.

His phone beeped, letting him know he had a text. He checked it and saw her email address. "Got it. I'll have to send it from my computer later."

"I can't wait." And she looked like she meant it. "Where do you get your ideas?"

He shrugged. "They just come to me. I have a whole list of potential plots, and I doubt I'll live long enough to write them all."

She shook her head. "I can't even imagine. I had to write a short story for a class in school once, and it was worse than pulling teeth. There's no way I could write a whole novel."

"And I could never teach dance," he said. "I think it's about passion."

Jasmine nodded. "I'll bet you're right."

The waitress came by and took their orders and then moved to the next table.

"You never really answered my question. So, where *do* you get your ideas?" Jasmine asked. "I'm really curious."

Zachary shrugged. "They just come to me. Sometimes something will spur me on, like a movie or a song. Maybe even a news story or a magazine headline. It just takes one little spark, and before you know it, it's a whole story with characters and everything."

"I don't know how you do it." She stared at him in amazement.

"That's what people always say," Zachary said. "But I think it just takes practice. I've been writing stories ever since I could spell enough words to string together a sentence."

She looked at him like he was a hero. His heart swelled, not used to that kind of attention.

"I've always like reading," she said, "even though I haven't made much time for it lately. I love how an entire world can be created through the use of just words."

Zachary nodded. "It's magical."

"I couldn't agree more." She looked thoughtful.

"Sometimes I find it hard to believe that there are only twenty-six letters, but yet with those few keys, so many different worlds and characters can be invented. The possibilities for story lines is endless."

"I never thought about it like that," she said, her voice low. "And I can't believe I'm hanging out with a real author."

He frowned. "I'm not published."

"You will be." She looked like she really believed it.

Six

JASMINE LOOKED INTO ZACHARY'S EYES from across the table. "Promise you'll email your book over as soon as you get home? I'm going to find out how to get the file on my tablet."

He nodded, still holding her gaze. "I will."

"Tell me more about the story," she said, resting her chin on her palms. It made her heart flutter when his face lit up as he talked about writing.

Zachary blushed. "I don't want to give too much away."

Jasmine pretended to pout. "Oh, okay." She paused with dramatic flair and then changed the subject. "Are you free tomorrow?"

It was strange being the one to initiate dates, but with Zachary, she didn't mind. He was like a hidden cove of jewels, and as he shared a little more about himself, it was like slowly opening a treasure chest. There was a fun and exciting person underneath the quiet and mysterious exterior.

"Sure," he said. "When are you free?"

"About the same as today. A couple hours around lunchtime and then in the evening."

He looked deep in thought. "I haven't walked along the beach since coming back to town. Would you want to do that around six-thirty? I'm having dinner with my family tomorrow night."

"Perfect. That sounds like a lot of fun." Jasmine couldn't believe he actually ate meals with his family. She had never even eaten with hers when living at home. Her parents couldn't stand each other, so they had long given up eating in the same room. In fact, they didn't bother making meals, period. She'd practically grown up eating microwave dinners in her bedroom with her homework as her only company.

They discussed where and when to meet, and then Zachary paid the bill, got up, and gave her his gorgeous smile.

Jasmine could have melted into a puddle over the table.

"Thanks so much for dinner," Jasmine said, standing. "I had a great time."

"Me, too." His smile widened. "Well, I'll see you tomorrow."

"I wouldn't miss it."

Zachary nodded and then walked away.

She watched him through the window until he was out of sight. He was something else. Clearly shy, but somehow that made him all the more attractive. It was hard to know what to make of him, but she couldn't wait to put the pieces together and see the full picture.

His book was a thriller, so obviously, he had a sense of adventure. Though he seemed reserved, there was clearly a thirst for life and action. Her pulse raced, wanting to figure out what exactly that meant.

He also wasn't her usual type, and that made him all the more exciting. She wanted to know more about him, to figure him out, and help him open up. Once he warmed up to her, he would probably be as talkative and excitable as anyone else. He was just one of those people who needed some time and encouragement.

One of her best friends in high school had been like that. Shy and reserved, always keeping to herself, but Jasmine had helped draw her out of the shell. Then the two of them had had a blast those four years, getting into more trouble than most of the popular kids.

Jasmine looked back from the window and realized the waitress was eying her. She'd been at the table daydreaming for a while. She picked up her purse and went outside, hit by the warm air after being in the air conditioned restaurant. She stood in the sun thinking about how Kate expected her to meet for the nightly concert.

Jasmine wasn't in the mood, and besides, she'd told Zachary she would read his story right away. With any luck, by the time she got back to the condo, his book would be waiting for her. She needed to figure out how to get it on a reading app.

She walked to the condo, barely paying attention to anyone or anything around her. Her steps felt lighter as she thought about Zachary. Even though she'd just met him the day before, she'd never felt this way about anyone. She was falling fast—but didn't care.

It was about time she did something crazy. There wasn't much left of the summer, and she deserved some fun before returning to Portland and landing a position at a prestigious dance studio.

Without realizing it, Jasmine already made it to the condo. She typed the security code into the box and went inside, digging the door keys from her purse. She entered, not surprised to find it empty. Kate was likely at the beach, flirting up a storm.

Jasmine kicked off her shoes and tossed her purse on the coffee table before going back to her room and turning on her laptop. The thing had been neglected most of the summer. It started slowly.

Probably making me pay for ignoring it, she thought, shaking her head.

Jasmine opened her email and didn't see one from Zachary, but it would be there soon enough. He probably had to take time to send it out, whatever that involved. She caught up on the emails she'd been avoiding for a while.

There was one from her mom, sent about a week

earlier trying to dig up dirt on her dad—her mom was always looking for a reason to leave him, but never did. Other emails showed family drama with some cousins. Jasmine rubbed her temples. Why did everyone try to drag her into their squabbles?

How she'd come from such a screwed up family, she'd never know. The only thing she was certain about was that she would continue working to not end up like them. If she ever ended up with a marriage like her parents had… she didn't even want to think about it.

Still no email from Zachary, so she jumped on a few of the social media sites to see what her friends were up to. At least she didn't have to worry about her family drama there. Jasmine refused to connect with any of them—there was no way she would let her friends see the crazy drama her family could stir up.

She'd made that mistake once, and wouldn't do that again. Some people had no business being online to share their problems with the world, and unfortunately, she was related to most of them.

After nearly a half an hour of getting nothing done, she checked her email again one more time. When she saw that there was still nothing from Zachary, she decided to get a shower and get ready for bed. He probably had better things to do than run home and send her a file, anyway.

He at least was close to his family from the sounds of it, and if they lived in town, he could easily be busy with them. Or he probably had friends and other things to do. She scolded herself for being so ridiculous expecting the story soon. And maybe he'd had second thoughts about sending it to her.

Sure, they seemed to be hitting it off and everything, but they barely knew each other. For all he knew, she might try to steal his story. Of course she wouldn't, but he didn't know that.

After a long shower, followed by a mud mask and new nail polish, she checked her computer once more. It still wasn't there, so she settled in on the couch, actually glad for a quiet night for a change. The nightly concerts were pretty fun, but some time to herself was necessary once in a while.

Jasmine found a romantic comedy and watched it while checking her email obsessively on her phone. Just after it ended, she heard the sounds of the keys in the door.

Kate stumbled in, her hair a mess and dark circles under her eyes. "You've been here all night?" she asked Jasmine.

"Yep."

"What have you been doing?" she asked. "That date didn't work out?"

"It was great."

Kate looked around. "Where is he?"

Jasmine raised an eyebrow. "Not here. What do you think I am? It was a first date."

"Well, what did you guys do?" Kate closed and locked the door.

"We had dinner."

"That's it?" asked Kate.

Jasmine nodded. "Yeah, and it went well."

"But it ended after you ate?" Kate didn't sound impressed.

"Right," Jasmine said. "He was—"

"Boring?"

"Not even close." Jasmine exhaled, her heart warming as she thought of Zachary. "You should see him. He's adorable… well, you'd say hot. He's both. He's kind of geeky and has a sweet charm."

"But he's sexy?" Kate asked, her face lighting up.

"Yeah, totally. I ran into him at the gym… actually, he ran into me." Jasmine giggled, remembering their meeting. "Oh, his smile. You should see it. He just… oh, I can't even explain it."

"You're flustered, Jas." Kate smiled.

"Completely and thoroughly."

"So sweet." Kate plopped on the couch next to her. "Tell me more."

"He's a writer. He's got a novel he's already finished and waiting to publish."

"In other words, he's unemployed." Kate put her feet on the coffee table, knocking over Jasmine's handbag.

Jasmine scowled. "How did you pull that out of

what I said? No. He's a *writer*. Not out of work."

"Unpublished. What does he do for a living?" Kate asked.

"I...."

"See? Unemployed."

Jasmine's stomach twisted in knots. "No, he isn't. Besides, aren't most of the guys *you* hang out with out of work?"

"I don't bother asking. It's not like any of them are boyfriend material."

"Then why bother hang out with them?" Jasmine asked.

"For a good time."

Jasmine was beginning to see that food choices weren't the only thing she and her roommate felt differently about. Granted, she'd known they had plenty of other differences, but it seemed so obvious now that Kate was judging Zachary without even meeting him.

"You'll have to ask him about his income next time you get together," Kate said. "Is there a next time? Since the date ended after dinner?"

"Of course, not that his income matters." Jasmine clenched her fists.

"Are you serious about him?"

Jasmine could feel defensiveness rising. She took a deep breath. "I just met him."

"Doesn't mean you can't be serious."

"What's with you?" Jasmine snapped. "Can't you

just be happy I met someone I like?"

Kate shrugged. "Sure. Just trying to figure out what's going on."

"Nothing. Why are you being so aggravating?"

"I'm not." Kate gave her a funny look. "Just trying to find out more about this guy, that's all."

"If you can't be positive, then just stop, okay? I want to enjoy being happy."

"Sure. Where's he from?"

"Here."

"A local boy?" Kate asked, appearing interested. "I've heard they can be trouble."

"Anyone can be, no matter where they live. He's sweet. You'll have to meet him." *That way you can stop judging him without seeing him*, Jasmine wanted to add.

"Okay. When?" Kate asked. "I'll find myself a date and we can make it a double."

Jasmine started to feel better. "I'll talk to him and let you know. But I'm going to bed now. It's getting late, and I have to go over my lesson plans before my classes tomorrow."

"Knock yourself out. I don't know why you bother with the plans."

"Haven't we been over this?" Jasmine asked. "I want to—"

The buzzer rang from the outside door.

"Are you expecting someone?" Kate asked.

Jasmine shook her head. "Nope."

"Me, neither." Kate walked over to the box and pressed the talk button. "Yes?"

"Is this where Jasmine Blackwell lives?"

Jasmine's stomach dropped to the floor. She knew that voice anywhere.

Kate turned around and gave her a questioning look. She let go of the talk button. "Who's that, and should I let her in?"

"It's my mom," Jasmine said, feeling nauseated. "I have no idea how she even found me."

Seven

~

ZACHARY STARED AT HIS LAPTOP, typing random letters on the keyboard. His parents watched the TV in their recliners while he was supposed to be working on his second novel. Their new agreement was that if he wanted to live with them he either needed to be actively working on his novels or get a job.

"It's not that we're not happy about having you here," his mom had said. "We're thrilled. The whole time you were away, we felt like a piece of our hearts were missing. Right, Robert?"

"Of course," his dad had agreed. "Between losing Sophia and my health problems last year, you boys mean more to us than ever. Having you here means more than you could know. We had only one child left here in Kittle Falls last year, and now we have all you boys except Rafael, and you know how hard your mom is working on bring him back to town."

Zachary shook his head. "I know how much effort she put into trying to bring me home."

"It goes double for Rafael now that he's the last one," his dad said. "She doesn't have to split her time between you and him anymore."

"I'm sure he's excited about that," Zachary said.

The conversation had moved back to the rules of living at home, but unfortunately, now as he tried to work on his novel, Zachary couldn't focus on it. He couldn't get his mind off Jasmine. She was gorgeous and seemed into him—for some reason. It was nice to have someone interested in him. And she actually cared about his book. Who else had asked to read it?

Guilt tugged at him for not sending the book file yet. He'd told her he would, but he couldn't bring himself to send it. What if she didn't like it? Of course, he would have to get over that fear if—no, when—he finally got published. Then, anyone would be able to read his work and look into his soul.

In some ways, putting his book out there was more of a risk than shouting his most embarrassing secrets for all to hear. There were parts of the story that expressed things he had no way of saying otherwise, and yet on the other hand, it had things in it that had nothing to do with him. The antagonist, for example. He was a horrible person who said and did terrible things Zachary despised. What if people thought that was how he thought deep down?

He sighed. It was no wonder he hadn't made it to being published yet. It would be too much. What if he wasn't cut out for this life like he thought? The thought of sending it out to just one person made his mouth dry and his pulse race.

Or was it because he cared what she thought? After dealing with Monica, he hadn't been sure if he would ever let a girl back in. It wasn't worth the risk. He'd rather be single if that was the case. He also loved his alone time, so it was a good excuse to just have all the time he needed.

But now that he'd met Jasmine, he couldn't help wondering if a relationship could actually work. If someone like her actually had an interest in his writing, it was possible. Writing wasn't just a job he went to and came home, able to ignore after leaving. No, it was part of him. If someone said they cared about him but didn't care about his writing, he had to question how they really felt about him.

He'd had old friends from school that he hadn't seen in years show more interest in reading his book than Monica ever had. That should have been his first clue to ditch her.

Zachary's phone beeped, and he checked to see who would text him. His heart raced when he saw Jasmine's name, and it went even faster as he pushed the button to read the text.

Just want to make sure I didn't miss your email. Can't wait to read your book.

His heart sank. He'd let her down—she'd probably been waiting since they left the restaurant. Or maybe she really just was checking to see if she'd missed the email… that he hadn't even sent.

Pulse pounding in his ears, Zachary texted her back.

I'm about to send it. Hope you like it.

His finger hovered over the send button for a moment before he finally pushed it.

Awesome. I can't wait.

Zachary's heart felt like it was going to burst outside of his chest.

"Here goes nothing," he mumbled, closing out his writing program and opening his email. His fingers shook as he opened a new message and wrote a quick note to Jasmine before uploading the files. He wasn't sure which type of reader she had, so he sent her everything he had.

This time, his mouse hovered over the send button. He finally pushed it.

There. Now that was over. He'd sent it, and she was going to read it. What was the worst that could happen? She'd hate it and decide never to see him again? That was unlikely, and even if it did happen, at least he'd gotten one more person to read it.

That was more than he and his agent had been able to do the entire time he'd been in New York. And

Jasmine was a nice person. If she didn't like it, she would probably tell him what he could do to improve it. Either way, he was one step closer to being a real author. Not just a writer, but someone with a novel that another person had actually read.

Just sent it. Let me know if it doesn't show up.

His phone beeped again.

Got it. Can't wait to start. A string of celebrating smilies danced following the words.

Zachary couldn't help smiling. Maybe this actually was a good thing.

He sent her some animated smilies also, not quite able to find anything to say.

Taking a deep breath, he waited to see if she sent anymore messages. After a minute, there was nothing. That must mean she was sending the file to her reader.

The urge to start the outline finally hit. He set his phone down and went back to his laptop and started typing about his second book. He started by writing out main ideas he already had. It wasn't much, but he could flesh it out once he had it written out. He read through what he had and thought of a few more ideas.

His phone beeped again, and when he checked the text, Jasmine had sent a screen-shot of the first page of chapter one. His heart jumped into his throat and then swelled with excitement. What a rush that she was so excited, but at the same time, it was the scariest thing he'd ever experienced.

Zachary thought of a bunch of things he could text back, but they all seemed too stupid. But he couldn't send nothing, either, so he finally settled on sending some reading emoticons. Thank goodness for those.

"What are you doing over there?" his mom asked, giving him a funny look.

"Discussing my book with someone."

She nodded. "I wondered what was so funny."

He went back to his outline and pushed away all other thoughts, especially the ones wondering what Jasmine thought of his story. Before too long, or at least what felt like it, he had several pages written out. He felt like he had enough meat to get started.

Zachary read it over, making sure there was enough of a character arc, a good enough set of antagonists, and some decent external and internal goals that would be thwarted often enough to keep things interesting. He made a few notes and then started planning out the details of the first several chapters.

Getting started was the hardest part—the long list of unwritten books on his notepad was evidence of that—but he finally felt ready to tackle this one. He wasn't sure how well the romance would work in the storyline, but he'd at least try. The worst that could happen would be having to rewrite that part.

He opened a blank page for the first chapter. It stared at him for a few minutes as he thought about the opening line. It had to be compelling. Something that would grab the reader and make them want to keep reading.

No pressure.

Zachary went back to his outline and read over the early parts and finally just decided to write. As long as he had something down, that was better than nothing. Unwritten words can't be edited, but even the worst written words could be. He could go back and fix the opening later.

After the first few paragraphs, he found his flow and was brought back into the world he'd created. Everything felt natural, almost like returning home. He'd spent so much time on the first book, he knew his main character almost better than he knew himself. Sure, he'd plunked Damion in a different country this time and with someone new who wanted him dead, but it was familiar enough that the words practically wrote themselves.

By the time he was ready for a break, he had a solid first chapter. He backed everything up even though it had automatically saved to the cloud. A writer can never have too many backups. He closed the laptop and set it next to him on the couch before getting up to stretch his legs and arms.

His parents had left the living room, but Zachary hadn't even noticed. That was a good sign—that he'd been so wrapped up in his writing that the world around him had disappeared. Now he just needed to keep that momentum going until he had another thirty or so chapters.

He went to the kitchen for a snack and found his mom making dessert.

"You've been typing for quite a while," she said, pouring chocolate sauce over ice cream. "I'm proud of you, Zachary. I knew you could get back into your rhythm."

"Hopefully, this will be the one. If anyone will even look at it."

She added sprinkles. "I'm sure it will be. The thing to remember is that you've already done something most people haven't. You've written a book and had others read it. It's brave."

He shrugged, sticking his thumbs into his pockets. "I wouldn't say that."

"I would."

She turned and looked him in the eyes. "I used to write stories when I was younger, but I never once let anyone read them. Not even your dad knows about them."

"You've written?" he asked, surprised.

"They're nothing much, but I did enjoy writing when I was younger."

"How come you never told me?" he asked.

She brought out a bag of small candies from the cupboard. "Because I'm nowhere near as daring as you.

You have guts, and I couldn't be more proud."

His face heated up. "Even though I'm not published?"

"Of course."

"Even though I went to New York and came back a failure?" He looked away.

She turned back to him and stepped closer. "I don't ever want to hear you say that again. You went after your dream, and though nothing has come of it yet, you're still pursuing it. The only way to fail is if you give up, and I don't see you doing that."

"Hopefully, I won't have to."

"Don't you know most success stories have a string of so-called failures behind it?" she asked. "It's all just a stepping stone to the great things ahead of you."

When had his mom become so wise? He nodded, feeling even more invigorated. "Yeah, you're right. Once one of these books gets picked up, so will the rest."

"Exactly. Don't let anyone else determine your worth. You show them. Make them regret ever turning you away."

Zachary nodded. "That's exactly what I'm going to do."

Eight

JASMINE HIT SNOOZE FOR ABOUT the eighth time and considered calling in sick. She wasn't, but she'd stayed up half the night reading Zachary's book. The first couple chapters were a little slow, but then when she hit the third one, it took off like an explosion, and she couldn't put it down.

Finally, her eyes wouldn't stay open another moment. Unfortunately, that was only four hours ago. She couldn't let that get the best of her. She still needed to be responsible and teach her classes. Sure, she could let a sub take over for the day, but that could show up on her file, making her look bad for the dance studios she wanted to get into.

She'd just have to drink coffee. A lot of it. Her habit had been to pick something up at a stand on her way to the club, but she needed some just to get ready this morning. They had some instant coffee that would work in a pinch—and that was what this was.

When she got to the kitchen and warmed up the

water, she turned around and jumped. She'd forgotten about her mom's arrival the night before. Now she slept on the couch, and no surprise, empty bottles of alcohol were strewn about on the floor.

Jasmine hoped that Kate hadn't seen the mess, and probably hadn't since she usually slept in, having signed up for later classes that Jasmine. Groaning, Jasmine gathered her mom's bottles and put them in the recycle. She would have to empty it on her way out before Kate could see them.

With any luck, her mom would sleep through the morning, and neither Kate nor she would have to deal with her mom. Then her mom could spend the afternoon working off her hangover, and possibly—but not likely—be pleasant when Kate and Jasmine got back home to the condo that night.

Jasmine didn't even know why her mom was in Kittle Falls. She'd tried to find out the night before, but it had been useless. Whatever the reasons, her mom wasn't ready to talk about them.

She couldn't help but wonder if her parents were finally splitting up. Growing up, she had waited, expecting the ball to drop any day, but they continued to stick out despite all the screaming and threats. It was why Jasmine had spent more nights at friends' houses than at her own home. No one seemed to notice or care, so it worked out well for everyone.

Or at least it seemed that way. Jasmine had thought

once she got out of the house she was done with all the drama. She hadn't seen her family since high school graduation, and she hadn't missed them. She felt guilty about that. Who wouldn't? They were her parents, and she wanted to have a good relationship with them, but they brought her down so much it wasn't worth it.

The little bit of counseling she'd had confirmed that much. Her parents would continue to drag her down as long as she let them. Jasmine's personal boundaries were the one thing she could give them that might help them to wake up and make the fixes they needed. And she had no intentions of holding her breath.

She just did her best to avoid alcohol, except to have a sip or two socially on occasion, so she wouldn't risk ending up like them. If anyone knew how alcohol could ruin lives, it was her. Jasmine couldn't even bring herself to think about her brother most days. Carter had followed in their parents footsteps, but he hadn't been so lucky.

One night—technically, early one morning—Carter had left a party and ran into a pole. Everyone said his death had been instant, but Jasmine thought they just said that so it would hurt less. It didn't.

The tea kettle hissed, letting her know the water was ready. She grabbed it off the stove so it wouldn't wake anyone, and made some instant coffee. She'd made it too strong and it tasted awful, but it would have to do. As long as it helped her heavy eyelids, she had no choice.

She drank half her mug, watching her mom sleep on the couch. How could her brother's accident not have been a wakeup call for parents? Instead of realizing how they'd messed up everything and sobering up, they'd only gotten worse—and she hadn't thought that was possible.

Jasmine had been the only one with the resolve to stay away from the poison. Now she needed to figure out what was going on with her parents. She needed to either send her mom back home or to rehab. She wasn't going to do anything to encourage her behavior, and based on the bottles she'd just picked up, her mom had no intentions of improving.

There was no time for that now, and her mom would likely sleep all day, anyway. She might not even wake up until Jasmine got back after work. Then she would insist they talk, or she would send her mom back home. She'd pay for a cab if needed.

She quickly got ready, drinking down the disgusting coffee as she went. Then she took the recycling down to the main canister downstairs. Though Kate would likely smell alcohol on her mom, she at least wouldn't see the evidence.

Back at the condo, she finished her coffee, grabbed her purse, and left. She went to the first coffee stand on her way and ordered a double shot latte. It tasted much better than the disaster she'd made earlier.

The coffee had Jasmine buzzing with energy despite

still feeling tired. Her eyelids were heavy, and she hadn't been able to hide the dark circles under her eyes with makeup.

When she arrived in her classroom, some kids were already waiting. She got them busy with warm-ups while she looked over her lesson plan for the day.

The morning breezed by as she sipped her latte. It kept her going, but she knew she'd need more by lunchtime. Her mind was already going at double speed, yet she couldn't stop yawning. It was an annoying combination. But at least she was able to think about what to do about her mom while she instructed the girls.

Lunch came around and Jasmine realized she'd forgotten to pack anything to eat. She went over to the window and grabbed her purse. She saw Zachary sitting in what was becoming "his" spot on the bench.

Her heart raced. She needed food to get through the rest of the day, but she wanted to see him more. She looked over the classroom and then left, hurrying to meet him.

As she approached, he set his tablet down and smiled. Oh, that smile. She couldn't get enough of it, and even better, it made her forget everything else.

She sat next to him, so close they were almost touching.

"I love your book," she said. "In fact, I'm running on fumes because I read it way too late last night."

His eyes widened. "Really?"

"I'm dying to know what happens to Damion. I would have stayed up to finish it if I could have skipped work."

Zachary's beautiful smile widened. "I'd tell you, but it would ruin the surprise."

"No spoilers." She laughed.

"How far did you get?" he asked.

"Damion just discovered the clue in the jewelry store."

"The one in Vienna?" Zachary asked.

Jasmine raised an eyebrow. "Vienna? When does he—?"

"I've said too much." He covered his mouth, his eyes shining.

"Oh," Jasmine complained. "Don't do this to me. How does he get there? I mean, with the broken leg and the—"

"You said no spoilers."

"I did. You're going to kill me." She shook her head. Her stomach rumbled—luckily not loud enough for him to hear. "Are you up for lunch? I forgot to pack mine. That's what I get for staying up too late."

"Sure, and it's my treat since it's apparently my fault." He grinned again. Jasmine loved the way his entire face lit up with his smile. "Sound good?"

Heat crept into her cheeks as she realized she'd been staring like a fool. "I'd have a hard time saying no to that, but are you sure?"

"I wouldn't offer if I wasn't." Zachary stood and held out his hand. She took it and stood, sliding her fingers in between his. She liked the way his hand felt like it was made for hers. He squeezed her hand, smiling wider.

Jasmine's heart raced. "Where to?" she asked.

"I know of a little place only the locals know about. They have some delicious pasta dishes and desserts to die for."

She stared into his eyes. She didn't care where they ate as long she was with him, and she could keep him smiling. "That sounds perfect."

"And they tend to not be as busy, too, which is always a plus during the lunch rush."

They walked down a road Jasmine had never noticed before, taking turns through parts of town she didn't know existed. "Is this Kittle Falls' hidden secret?"

"We have a whole part of town that's ignored by the tourists, but since you've been here all summer, it doesn't really make you a visitor, does it?" He smiled, his eyes shining.

How did he expect her to answer when he looked at her like that?

Jasmine shook her head, sure he thought her a fool. She just couldn't find any words. Her skin felt afire, holding his hand and having him look at her that way. And even more amazing, he didn't seem put off by her looking like a wreck from so little sleep.

Zachary led her into a little diner that looked like it belonged in a television show from the fifties or sixties. It even had red and white checked tablecloths and a jukebox playing music from that era.

"This place is adorable," she said.

"I've always liked it." He led her to a table in a corner and held out a chair for her.

He was a gentleman, too? She sat, and he scooted her in before sitting next to her.

A waitress, looking like she was from the same time period as the diner, came over to them. "So good to see you again, Zachary. How can I help you, hon?" She pulled a pencil from behind her ear and a pad of paper from her apron.

"You, too. What's the daily special, Sheila?" Zachary asked.

"Our six-cheese ziti. But for you, anything. Are you back in town for good, or just visiting?" asked Sheila.

"I'm here for a while."

"Your parents must be thrilled. You boys are returning one by one. Who's this?" Sheila turned to Jasmine.

"This is Jasmine, and she's new to this side of town."

"You won't want to go back to the touristy side after you've been here." She winked at Jasmine. "Does the ziti sound good to you?"

"Sure." Jasmine shrugged.

"Two zitis, Sheila," Zachary said. "And can I get a root beer?"

Sheila scribbled on her pad of paper. "Sure, dear. And you?" She looked at Jasmine.

"Can I get a coffee? Black."

"Coming right up." She turned around and walked away.

"Sounds like you come in pretty often," Jasmine said.

"I used to come in a lot after school for snacks. This place hasn't changed a bit. My dad says it's the same since he was a boy, too."

"It's incredible that your family has been here that long."

Zachary shared stories about growing up while they waited for the food. When it arrived, Jasmine went for the coffee first. Even though she was sitting with the most handsome guy in town, she had a hard time fighting her heavy eyelids.

Nine

⁓

ZACHARY ATE HIS PASTA, HARDLY able to focus on anything other than Jasmine. She was so beautiful, though obviously tired. He knew he should feel bad about that, but couldn't stop smiling over her staying up late to read his book.

She kept asking questions about what it had been like growing up in Kittle Falls, and he answered each question, not feeling like it was all that exciting, but she seemed genuinely interested. He couldn't imagine what was so interesting about growing up in a small town where everyone knew everyone—even now. Sheila had worked at the diner as long as Zachary could remember.

"What was it like where you grew up?" he asked, tired of talking about Kittle Falls.

"Nothing like this." Jasmine took another sip of her coffee. It was already her second cup since arriving.

"Sorry you're so tired," Zachary said.

"Funny. You don't sound sorry." She grinned, her tired eyes shining.

"Well, I can't help being excited that you're tired because of my story."

"Hopefully, I can finish it tonight before it gets too late. I'm not sure I can do this again." She yawned. "But I do need to know what happens to Damion."

"It's a good thing we're having lunch rather than dinner." Zachary finished off his pasta. "Does this replace the beach walk we had planned?"

She appeared to think about it. "It would give me time to finish the book. Is that okay?"

Zachary felt his face warm. As much as he wanted to spend more time with her, excitement rushed through him—she wanted to finish his novel! He fought to keep his voice steady. "Of course."

"Though, we do need to have dinner soon," she said. "My roommate wants to meet you."

"You've told her about me?" Zachary arched a brow, surprised. She liked him enough to tell her roommate about him?

Jasmine nodded, and then took another sip of her coffee.

"How about after you finish my book?" he asked. "Then we don't have to worry about you staying up too late."

"I'd like that. But if that doesn't happen by tomorrow, do you want to do lunch again? It seems like a good time for the both of us."

"My schedule is flexible," Zachary said, "so whatever

works for you." Even if his schedule was packed, he'd rearrange it just to spend time with her.

"Okay, lunch tomorrow. Maybe dinner, too?" She looked hopeful.

"Sounds good to me." He could help grinning.

Sheila took their plates and then brought them desserts. "These are on the house. I'm so glad you're back in town, Zachary."

"Thanks so much, Sheila. You didn't have to."

"No, but I wanted to." She winked and then headed to another table.

Jasmine gestured to the sweets. "Do you want the banana split or the sundae?"

"Whichever you don't want."

She laughed. "I want both. They look delicious."

The two desserts were piled ridiculously high with ice cream and different colored syrups.

"We could always share them," he said. Normally, he wasn't one to share food, more worried about germs, but with Jasmine, he didn't care.

She beamed. "I like the way you think, Mr. Creativity."

They dug into the ice cream, and before Zachary knew it, both were gone and Sheila brought out the check. He pulled out his wallet, knowing he would have to find a way to earn money so he could keep taking Jasmine out. He'd arrived in town nearly broke, and now most of those measly funds were depleted.

"I've got this one," Jasmine said.

"But I should—"

"Pay for everything?" she asked. "Nonsense." She pulled a card out of her purse, put it on top of the receipt, and set at the edge of the table.

"Well, thanks," he said. "I'll get it next time."

"Deal."

They discussed possible restaurants for their next date until Sheila returned and the bill had been paid. Then he took her hand, noticing his pulse had picked up speed at the touch of her soft, warm skin. When they walked outside, a light breeze blew, and the scent of her perfume tickled his nose. He loved it—it was sweet, just like her.

He moved closer to her so he could smell it some more. Her soft, thick hair brushed against him and he wanted to reach over and run his hands over it.

All too soon, they were back at the club.

Jasmine turned and looked him in the eyes. "I have to get back and get ready for my next class."

"Me, too. Well, I have to meet my brother soon to work out, so I can't stay, either."

Jasmine squeezed his hand, and Zachary's heart raced. They said quick goodbyes, walking slowly away from each other. Zachary watched her until she disappeared through the door, wishing they could spend the rest of the afternoon together. He'd have to find out what she was doing over the weekend. They could go to the beach and spend the day together, not having to let each other go until they'd had hours and hours together.

But that would take money, even if she insisted on paying for some of it. He'd have to talk to his parents or Jake about working at the family shop part time. Or if they didn't need help, then he would have to figure something else out. He did have credit cards, but he didn't want to put himself into debt.

Maybe Brayden needed some help with his clinic. His urgent care facility was almost ready to open, but still needed some work. Maybe there was something he could do to help. That reminded him, he needed to get inside and meet his brother.

When he got there, Brayden was already stretching.

"You look happy," Brayden said, pulling his arm above his head and grabbing his elbow.

Zachary put his stuff in an empty locker. "Maybe I am."

"Oh, good." His oldest brother looked genuinely pleased. "Is it your book?"

"I met a girl," Zachary said. "A nice one this time." He reached his arm over his head and pulled on it with the other hand.

"It sounds like anyone would be better than the last one." Brayden stretched his leg.

Zachary rolled his shoulders. "No, it wouldn't take much to improve upon her, but Jasmine is really wonderful."

"Oh?" Brayden switched legs. "Where'd you guys meet?"

"Here, actually."

Brayden looked around the weight room.

"Not here, here." Zachary laughed. "She's a dance instructor in the club."

"Maybe she can help you out."

"What's that supposed to mean?" Zachary asked.

Brayden laughed. "You've never been one with great moves."

"You don't like my dancing?"

Brayden slapped him on the back. "Let's just say your talents lie elsewhere."

Zachary shook his head. "I can always count on my brothers."

"Who cares about dancing when you're going to be a famous author?" Brayden picked up some dumbbells and started reps.

"I don't know about that, but Jasmine does like my novel."

"See?" Brayden asked. "You'll be famous, you just have to give it time. Remember, Walt Disney was turned down for a job at a newspaper because they said he lacked creativity. Some people don't know talent even if it bites them in the butt. So, the girl, she has good taste. Stick with her."

Zachary grabbed a foot and stretched his leg. "Speaking of her. I'm going to need to start making some more money if I want to keep taking her out. Do you know if Mom and Dad need help at the shop? Or do you need help with anything for the clinic?"

"You live with them. Don't you know if they need help at the shop?" Brayden asked.

"I haven't asked yet. The thought just struck me on the way here." Zachary switched legs.

Brayden switched positions and did more reps. "I don't know about them, but I don't need any help right now. The final touches are being put on the building, and I'm hiring non-medical staff. I don't really want to hire you as a janitor, and I doubt you have receptionist skills."

"I wouldn't be good at either one. Well, maybe a receptionist. Is it similar to being a cashier at the shop?"

"Kind of, but a lot more paperwork."

Zachary thought about it. "But you probably need someone full time. I just need part time work."

"With the twenty-four hour clinic, I might have to take what I can get." Brayden put down the dumbbells. "Tell you what. You see what's needed at the shop, and I'll see what kind of openings I have left. I've actually hired someone to oversee the hiring so I don't have to."

Zachary picked up some dumbbells. "Sounds like a plan. Thanks, Brayden."

"Anytime." Brayden moved across the room to one of the weight machines.

Zachary did some reps, looking around the room.

The punching bag caught his attention, and he found that he didn't have so much negative energy this time. Things looked brighter already.

He finished his workout and then made his way back home, hoping to find out if he was needed at the shop. He'd worked there for a long time in high school. Surely, everything would come back once he started. Then he would have some money coming in so he could hopefully take Jasmine on a real date.

When he got inside the house, he heard conversation. At first, he thought his parents were talking with Cruz, but then Zachary realized that wasn't Cruz's voice.

He followed the voices into the kitchen.

"Rafael!" Zachary's eyes lit up. "What are you doing here?"

His older brother got up from the table and they embraced.

Rafael patted him on the back. "Good to see you, Zachary."

"You, too. What a surprise. What brings you back to Kittle Falls?"

"Can't a man come back to his family without a reason?" Rafael asked.

"He hasn't told us yet, either," their dad said. He shot Rafael a mock-annoyed expression.

"I'd love to hear about it," Zachary said, "My aching muscles are begging me to sit, though."

Zachary sat at the table, and Rafael sat across from him. He took off what was clearly a designer coat and laid it on the chair next to him. Then he undid the top two buttons of a deep purple silk shirt.

"That's better," Rafael said. "I don't know why I didn't dress more comfortably. No, that's not true. I wanted to fit in with the other first class passengers." He shrugged.

Zachary shook his head. "You'd fit in if you wore a t-shirt and shorts."

Rafael raked his fingers through his hair, looking as tired as Jasmine had. "Surely, you're not suggesting I would wear cotton?"

"Of course not." Then Zachary looked down at his own clothes—all cotton. "So, what brings you back home?"

"You people aren't going to give up, are you?" Rafael asked.

"Of course not," said their dad, glancing up from his crossword puzzle.

"Welcome home," Zachary said. He sniffed something sweet in the air. Peaches. "Do I smell Mom's famous cobbler?"

She smiled, getting up from the table. "Of course. All our boys are in town. It's cause for celebration."

Zachary raised an eyebrow. "Are you here to stay, Raf?"

"More like an extended vacation." Rafael repositioned himself in the chair and then sipped from a wine glass. "I had some... creative differences with my business partner."

"And now you're here?" Zachary asked. That didn't sound like Rafael.

"We agreed to part ways, and he bought out my share." Rafael took another sip.

"But you started the business," their dad said, sitting up taller. "Why did he get to keep it?"

"He didn't keep it," Rafael said, taking another sip. "He bought me out. But Tony took it to the next level in ways I never could. That's why I wanted to go into business with him. Things were going fabulous, but then it became clear we had different plans for the company, and we couldn't make it work moving in two different directions."

"Why did you sell out?" asked their mom.

"I've been thinking about returning since Dad was in the hospital," Rafael said. "I hate being away from everyone, and now even more so, knowing you're all here. My disagreements with Tony were the push I needed to make the move back. My plan is to start something up here. It might not do as well as in LA, but at least I'll be back home with everyone."

"But you said an extended vacation... does that mean you're staying?" Their mom looked at him with a hope-filled expression.

"I do need to return to LA at some point to tie up

some loose ends," Rafael said, "but pretty much, I'm here to stay. I've been looking at real estate online and there are a few homes on the outskirts of town I'd like to look at."

"We have our family back," said their mom, her eyes filling with tears.

Ten

≈

JASMINE OPENED THE DOOR TO her condo, her mind stuck on Zachary. The kids made fun of her all afternoon for being in her own world, but since that was where Zachary was, she didn't mind putting up with the playful teasing.

The sight in front of her brought her back to reality—too much and too quickly. The couch was covered in empty bottles, but her mom was nowhere to be seen.

"Mom?" Jasmine called.

Silence.

Maybe Jasmine would be lucky and her mom had decided to leave town already. She put her purse down near the door and gathered the empty bottles, taking them back down to the recycle for the second time that day.

When she got back up to the condo, she thought about what to tell her mom. It wouldn't be easy, but she would need to kick her out unless she sobered up. Jasmine also needed to find out what she was doing in

Kittle Falls and how long she planned on staying. Her mom hadn't told her anything.

Jasmine checked the couch for spills and cleaned up the ones could see. It felt like she was back home again. Cleaning up after her mom brought back more memories than she cared to think about—when her parents should have been caring for her and yelling at her not to drink alcohol, the roles had been reversed.

Tears stung her eyes, but she blinked them away. She'd decided long ago to stop feeling sorry for herself and her ruined childhood. She had made it up to herself by having a blast with her dancing career and moving around the country without a care in the world, traveling from one production to the next as it suited her.

Now her past was back in her face, and if she wasn't careful, Kate would know everything. Jasmine had done so much to keep her family life and troubles a secret from her new friends and to separate her new life from the old one.

After she had cleaned up all her mom's messes—including dirty plates with caked-on food that hadn't made it into the sink—she looked through the condo to see if her mom had decided to crash on a bed. Thankfully not. Her bags still sat by the front door, so Jasmine knew she would be back at some point.

Her stomach rumbled, so she went to the fridge. All the food was gone, only leaving ketchup and a tiny amount of milk in the jug.

"Thanks, Mom," Jasmine muttered sarcastically. She'd even eaten Kate's food.

Jasmine slammed the fridge shut and snatched her purse. She would have to go grocery shopping and replace the food her mom had eaten. Either her mom hadn't eaten for days or she had the munchies, which meant she was doing more than just drinking. Not that that was a huge surprise.

Anger building, she stormed out of the condo. It only took a minute before she was furious. Everything flooded back from her childhood, only fueling her anger further. She thought she was done with her parents—there had been a reason she didn't keep in touch or tell them where she was.

Jasmine would find out who told her mom where she was and give them an earful. No one had a right to tell anyone anything about her, much less give out the address of where she stayed.

By the time she got back to the condo with her arms loaded with groceries, she was ready to scream at someone. Jasmine didn't even care if she caused a scene. After everything she'd been through, her mom had no right to waltz back into her life.

Everything was going well, she didn't need her mom ruining any of it. Her internship was going better than she had hoped, and now she'd even met a wonderful guy with sticking potential—at just the time she was ready to think about a serious relationship.

Why did her mom have to come back and potentially ruin everything? She and her dad had already done enough damage. Would they not stop until they killed her, too?

Jasmine threw all the groceries into the fridge and cabinets, not even caring if she broke something. She'd probably have to buy more the next day if her mom decided to stay, anyway.

She wanted to call her dad and find out what was going on, but she didn't even have their number anymore. She'd heard through the grapevine that they'd moved a couple times since she'd graduated—probably evicted for not paying rent or for trashing the place. Or maybe both.

Pacing, Jasmine thought about what she would say to her mom when she returned. She had many choice words, but wasn't sure what the best way to handle it was. Start out nice and then get mean? Or just jump right into how she felt? Part of her wanted to lay her mom out for everything she'd done over the years.

She had ruined so many lives, but she probably didn't even realize it. She never had before. Why should she start now? Jasmine paced more furiously.

Kate walked in and her eyes widened, watching Jasmine pace. "Is everything okay?"

"Does it look like it?" Jasmine snapped.

"That would be negative. Want to talk about it?"

"No," Jasmine fumed. "I need to take it out on my

mom."

"What's her deal? Was she drunk or something?" Kate asked. "She acted like she had a hangover this morning."

"Oh?" Jasmine asked. "She was actually awake in the morning hours? Why? So she could get an early start drinking?"

"I take it this isn't something new with her?" Kate asked.

"That would be correct."

"I always wondered why you never talk about your family."

Jasmine scowled. "Nothing to talk about." Jasmine continued pacing. "I need to kick her out."

"Maybe she needs help."

Jasmine laughed bitterly. "She doesn't want any. Trust me."

"What if she doesn't have anywhere to stay?" Kate asked. "Is that why she's here?"

"Not my problem. She's always relied on me, even when I was way too young for it. She's the most irresponsible parent on earth. Right next to my dad. When I was in high school, I worked, but I never got to see any of that money. No. It went straight into the rent. In fact, we were living in such pitiful housing that my lame part time job paid the entire rent each month." Jasmine didn't know why she was going off like that, but it felt good.

Kate raised an eyebrow. "Maybe it's time you guys talk it out."

"Oh, I intend to." Jasmine's eyebrows came together.

"Where is she now?" Kate asked.

"Probably at the nearest bar."

"Have you called your dad?" Kate asked.

Jasmine laughed. "It's bad enough that I have one of them to deal with. I'm not opening another can of worms. There's enough crazy here to last me a lifetime."

"I have a date for dinner. Do you want me to cancel so I can give you moral support?"

"You'd do that?" Jasmine stopped pacing.

"Of course." Kate frowned. "I can see how much this is upsetting you. I'll provide backup. She might think she can boss you around because she's your mom, but she won't dare mess with me. I'll have her in tears first."

Jasmine couldn't help smiling. "I appreciate that. Really, I do. But I don't want you here to witness it. It's not going to be pretty. She's going to wish she crashed somewhere else."

Kate stared at her, appearing deep in thought. "If you're sure. I don't mind sticking around, and I promise not to think less of you—if that's what you're worried about. Sometimes you just need a friend."

"She might not even come back tonight. Bars stay open until, what? Well after midnight?"

"Two or three, usually."

Jasmine shook her head. "Then she'll be drunk out of her mind, and that won't be the time to attempt a conversation. I may have to call in sick tomorrow just so I can deal with this.

"You haven't had to miss a day of your internship yet. Are you sure?"

"Once again, I have to put my life on hold because of her. Not only on hold, but put my job in jeopardy."

"I'd hardly call missing one day putting your internship on the line."

Jasmine paced again. "You're right. In fact, she won't even be up by then. I'll have to cancel my lunch date and come here to let her have it."

Kate frowned. "Want me to give it to her? Maybe it'll have more of an impact from an outsider."

"No, it's my job." Anger bubbled in Jasmine's stomach. She wanted to hit something, but she'd have to wait to let her anger loose until her mom showed up… whenever that would be. "Get ready for your date. I have a book to read, anyway. I'd rather focus on that than this. She's not worth my time or energy."

"If I see her in the morning, awake, do you want me to ask her what's going on?" Kate asked. "Maybe she'll tell me. She might know how you feel about her and not listen."

"She has no idea how I really feel—otherwise she wouldn't have even thought about showing her face here." Jasmine picked up her purse and without another word went into her room. She appreciated Kate's support, but she needed to be alone—desperately.

Jasmine paced for a bit before plunking down on the bed. She took several deep breaths, but didn't find it helped any. She tried breathing even deeper, but was too upset to manage anything other than shallow ones.

She pulled out her tablet and opened the app to read Zachary's novel. Her mind raced as she started reading, and she had to re-read the first paragraph three times before giving up. There was no way she could focus. At least not in this state of mind.

All thanks to her mom. She only had to show up, and magically—tragically—everything in Jasmine's life was ruined once again. Just like it always had been.

Jasmine picked up a pillow and threw it against the wall. Magical powers, indeed. She leaned against her remaining pillow and closed her eyes, trying to relax. It wasn't easy—a lot of old, forgotten memories surfaced. All kinds of fights and arguments, broken possessions, crushed dreams, and ruined lives.

Every memory of her brother sliced at her heart. She and Carter had spent so much time fighting themselves, having learned nothing else from their parents. But despite that, they had been tight, sticking up for each other both at home and school. They tended to get picked on because they would show up at school with dirty, torn clothes and messy hair—even sometimes when they were old enough to take care of that stuff themselves.

There had been too many days when the bus would show up when they had no time to run a brush through their hair after waking up to a soul-crushing fight between their parents, who shouted horrible names at each other. And sometimes the kids.

It made her feel like a helpless kid again, just thinking about it. Instead of being in her room, she was brought back to the cramped, smoky trailer with dark green, stained carpeting. Her dad lay on the torn couch, a beer in one hand and a cigarette in the other. Her mom let out a string of profanities from the kitchen. The smell of burnt food filled the room.

"Did you burn dinner again, woman?" her dad shouted.

"It's your fault, you lazy bum! You didn't clean your chewing tobacco off the stove. That's what burned."

"You blaming this on me? Don't go there. You'll regret it."

She came into the living room and threw a potholder at him. "Don't threaten me, you poor excuse for a man." Then she called him several more colorful names.

Carter dropped the toy train he was playing with against the wall. Jasmine watched his eyes widen as their gazes connected. He gestured for her to go back to their bedroom. It was his turn to deal with them, which meant she got to hide in the closet this time.

Without a word, Jasmine bolted past him and into their room. She climbed over her bed and opened the closet, closing it as quietly as she could. The foul words and name calling was so loud, she covered her ears and pressed herself as far back against the wall as she could.

Jasmine bumped into a stuffed dog. It was Carter's, but she held it tight, anyway. She sang a song from dance class, trying not to think about what was going on out in the living room. Sometimes pretending helped.

Glass broke. Jasmine jumped and squeezed the toy closer. Something crashed into a wall, and then Carter's sobs could be heard. He called someone horrible names. Then he let out a horrible wail that brought tears to Jasmine's eyes. She couldn't stay in her room—not this time.

She scrambled out, leaving the dog on her bed and ran into the living room. A large mirror that had been on the wall now lay in several pieces on the floor. Her mom had a welt near her eye. Carter was in their dad's hold, tears streaming down his face.

Jasmine ran for her brother, screaming. She pulled on him with all her might, and Dad was so drunk, he couldn't keep his hold. Jasmine dragged her older brother out the front door. They ran down the lane, huffing and puffing before long. Eventually, they came to an empty trailer that the kids often played in because the front door was broken.

"We'll stay in here until they pass out," Carter said.

"We'll be okay. I promise."

A noise in the hallway brought Jasmine back to the present. She kicked her feet—she didn't want to think about any of this. It was in the past—where it needed to stay. There wasn't anything she could do about any of it. It had happened, and it was over. Her parents had been drunk jerks, and her brother was dead.

Jasmine wished it had been her parents in the car that night instead of him. Tears streamed down her face as she fell into a fitful sleep.

Eleven

~

JASMINE WOKE TO THE SMELL of smoke. It was an all-too familiar scent, having filled her house growing up. Her parents had always sucked on various types of cigarettes between sipping alcohol. But this was different—it wasn't that kind of smoke.

The fire alarm went off, and she sat up. The noise wailed, hurting her ears. She looked around, seeing smoke coming from underneath the doorway. Her heart skipped a beat. She heard Kate screaming from somewhere in the condo.

Jasmine raced out of bed and ran to the door, opening it. The handle was warm to the touch and her heart sank. Smoke hit her in the face and she covered her mouth and nose with her arms, coughing. She ducked as she ran down the hall.

In the living room, she saw flames engulfing the couch and spreading toward the wall nearest her.

Her mom.

Jasmine rushed to the couch, not seeing her.

"Out here," Kate called from the hallway.

She ran out, finding Kate with her mom on the floor. Her mom looked around confused.

"Did you do this?" Jasmine shouted. "Get up! We have to get out of here."

"I had to drag her out here," Kate said.

Jasmine glared at her mom. "Why bother?"

"Get me to a hospital," her mom moaned.

"I think her arm's burned," Kate said. "She didn't wake until I pulled her off the couch."

"When are you going to get a clue?" Jasmine yelled. "Look at what you've done! You've started another fire. Will you never learn?"

Kate put her hands under Jasmine's mom's arms. "Grab her feet. We've got to get her downstairs."

Flames shot out of the condo, coming close to them.

Jasmine grabbed her mom's legs and headed for the stairs. Sirens wailed outside. They made it down the two flights of stairs and outside, where a crowd gathered, all in their pajamas. Jasmine and her mom were the only ones in regular clothes. Apparently, Jasmine had forgotten to change before lying down.

Medics ran over to them. "Are you ladies okay?" asked one.

"She's burned." Jasmine indicated toward her mom.

"I thought I put the cigarette out," she moaned.

"Looks like we know the cause of the fire." He shook his head and then turned to another medic. "Go get a stretcher."

Everything happened in a blur as her mom was loaded into the ambulance and all the other residents crowded around.

"Do you want to come with?" asked a medic.

Jasmine shook her head. "I don't want to get in your way. I'll go down later, after she's been taken care of." She backed up and stood with Kate as they watched the firefighters put out the blaze.

"I can't believe our condo went up in flames," Kate said, leaning against Jasmine. "All our stuff."

"Unfortunately, this isn't a first," Jasmine muttered.

"What are we going to do?" Kate asked.

Jasmine felt moisture on her shoulder. She wrapped an arm around her friend. "It'll be okay. Somehow."

Kate sniffed. "All my stuff."

"Mine, too." Jasmine shook her head. "Did we opt in for renters insurance? Do you remember?"

"I think it was required," Kate said.

"At least we have that."

"You know what?" Kate asked. "Did you notice the smoke detectors in our place didn't go off?"

Jasmine nodded. "It was the smoke that woke me. The alarm went off later."

Kate lifted her head. "Right. The ones in the hallway. Shouldn't the owners have been in charge of that? I bet we could sue. Get more than just our stuff replaced."

"They would turn around and sue us," Jasmine said.

"We agreed to no smoking inside."

"But your mom didn't, and she's the one who caused this."

"And we're the ones who let her in." Jasmine ran her fingers through her hair. "We won't have a leg to stand on." Why had she let her mom in the door? *Why?* She should have known it could only end up in tragedy. She hoped no one else ended up hurt from the flames or the smoke, or Jasmine would be to blame. She should have known better than to let her mom stay. When she'd buzzed the condo the other night, she should have had Kate lie and say she didn't know her.

Jasmine ran her hands down her side and felt something in her pocket. Her phone. She pulled it out, surprised to have even one of her possessions.

"If you need me, I'll be over there." Jasmine pointed to an area where no one stood.

Kate nodded, watching the firefighters.

Jasmine turned on the screen and did a quick online search to find her dad. It was easy enough because they never paid the fees to be unlisted—unlike Jasmine always did.

"Hello?" asked her dad, his voice slurring.

"Do you know where Mom is?" Jasmine demanded.

"Jas? Is that you?" His words continued to garble.

"It sure isn't Carter, now is it?" she snapped.

"Where are you?" he asked.

"I asked you a question. Do you know where Mom

is?"

"Uh… no. Want me to leave her a message?" he asked. Paper rustled in the background.

"No, actually, I don't. She's in the hospital."

"What? Where?" he asked.

"Did you even notice she was gone?" Jasmine asked. "This is the second night she's been on my couch, but the first that she set it on fire. The whole building, in fact. A lot of people have to find somewhere else to live thanks to her."

He let loose a long string of profanities. "Do I gotta come and get that woman?"

"Don't bother. You'd probably just kill an innocent bystander."

"What hospital?" he asked.

"Wouldn't you like to know?" Jasmine asked. "I'll tell you when you've sobered up."

"Sober? That could take—"

"A lifetime. Probably longer in your case. Just get the alcohol out of your system, and we'll talk later."

"She's been gone two nights, you said?" he asked.

"Quick as lightning, huh, Dad? Typical. Bye."

"Wait. What's your number? How can I—?"

"Still don't have caller ID?" Jasmine shook her head. Like that was a big shock. "I'll be in touch." She ended the call before he could engage her again.

She went back over to Kate, who had a tear-stained face.

"They got the fire out." Kate sniffed. "But they aren't letting anyone back in until they inspect the building. They don't know the extent of the damage, but my guess is all of our stuff is toast. Literally." Tears ran down Kate's face.

Jasmine hugged her, wishing she could find it in her to cry. But she'd cried a lifetime's worth of tears growing up. She rubbed her friend's back. "I'm really sorry, Kate. It's all my fault. I shouldn't have let her in."

"No, it's her fault. I *told* her she couldn't smoke, but she did it, anyway. You and me, we did all we could. I know you cleaned up after her and replaced the food she ate."

Anger rose again in Jasmine's chest. "You told her not to smoke? I hope they lock her away for life."

Kate stepped back, wiping her eyes. "Who'd you call over there? That guy you've been seeing?"

Jasmine shook her head. "My dad. He didn't even know she'd left."

Kate's eyes widened. "Seriously? But she's been here two days."

"And it probably took her a day or more to get here." Jasmine scowled.

"I can't believe you came from a family like that." Kate shook her head.

"That's the best compliment anyone could pay me," Jasmine said. "I've worked hard to stop the cycle of stupidity and actually do something with my life."

"I admire your work ethic even more now." Kate pulled some hair from her face and tucked it behind her ears.

"You admire me?" Jasmine asked, surprised.

"Why do you think I hang around you?" Kate asked. "I need some of your responsibility to rub off on me. I think it has. Don't you?"

Jasmine couldn't help yawning. "Where are we going to sleep tonight?"

"I heard people saying that there's some kind of shelter in a high school gym or something."

Hot, angry tears filled Jasmine's eyes. "None of this should have happened. All these people should be sleeping in their beds." She really did wish that her parents had perished rather than Carter that horrible night.

Kate put an arm around Jasmine. "Like you said, it's all going to be okay."

"Okay?" Jasmine asked, staring at the building. "I was wrong. All these people are out of a home."

"Ninety percent are here temporarily, like us. Tourists and summer renters."

"And the other ten?" Jasmine asked. She wanted to shake her mom.

"Without a home now." Kate frowned.

A couple police officers came over and said they needed to question everyone. Jasmine's stomach dropped to the ground, and she exchanged a look with her roommate. Kate nodded and then so did Jasmine. They would tell them everything.

Jasmine and Kate each went with a different cop, and Jasmine told him everything from her mom showing up uninvited to the empty bottles. She explained how Kate had told her not to smoke, but that she had, anyway, after she'd gone to bed. Then she made sure to mention how the smoke alarm inside the condo hadn't gone off.

The only thing she and Kate had done wrong was to try and help a desperate woman. Whether they wanted to charge her mom or the condo owner, it was up to them. The officer scribbled notes furiously on a pad of paper and then thanked Jasmine. Apparently, he didn't think they'd done anything wrong, either.

Jasmine let out a silent sigh of relief.

Once she and Kate were both done, one of the policemen explained how to get to the high school where cots and snacks were being set up.

Kate thanked him and then dragged Jasmine over to her car. "Do you want to go there or to the hospital?"

"I'm not hurt," Jasmine said. "Are you? Did you get burned dragging my mom off the couch?"

Kate shook her head. "You know what I mean. I realize you two don't have the best relationship, but maybe this will be a wakeup call for her. She could even hear you out finally."

"Like the last fire she started was a wakeup call? Or

when my brother died?" Jasmine shook her head, more tears building. "Nothing is going to get through to her. Nothing. The only way she'll stop drinking is if she's dead. Or paralyzed and can't lift a bottle to her face. But even then, she'll probably find a way. She's creative when she can't get her vices."

"Wait. Back up. Your brother...? I thought you were an only child."

"I am now. Let's go to the high school. I'll deal with my mom tomorrow."

Twelve

~

Zachary closed the story in his Kindle and checked the time. Maybe Jasmine had lunch at a different time today. He pulled out his phone and sent her a quick text.

Are we still on for lunch?

While he waited for the reply, he moved over to a bench in the shade. He hadn't anticipated waiting this long in the sun. His skin felt a little too warm. He probably should have worn sunscreen but had been more interested in stretching so he wouldn't be sore again. The soreness was finally waning as his body adjusted to regular workouts.

After five long minutes of no reply, he considered texting again. He didn't want to come off as pushy or needy, but he wanted to make sure everything was okay. What if something had happened?

He vaguely recalled hearing something about a fire near the beach. At the time, he hadn't thought anything of it—though he really should have. What if it had been a massive fire? Hadn't she said her condo was near there?

Zachary pulled out his phone and Googled the fire. Sure enough, it was a condo mostly rented by tourists and summer visitors like Jasmine. His pulse raced as he read the rest of the article. Someone who fell asleep with a cigarette had caused the blaze, destroying the unit as well as several others near it. All residents were sent to a high school where a temporary shelter was set up until the building was deemed livable or they could find somewhere else to stay.

He didn't care if he scared her off. It was time for another text.

Are you okay? Were you in the building that caught on fire?

While waiting, he got off the bench and paced. After a few minutes with no response, he couldn't take it anymore. He went inside the gym and looked into the room where she taught her classes. It was empty, but if she was on lunch, it would be, anyway.

I'm starting to worry. Can you just let me know if you're all right?

A lady walked by wearing a shirt with the gym logo. "Excuse me," Zachary said.

"Yes?" she asked, stopping.

"Do you know where Jasmine Blackwell is? She

teaches in that room."

"I don't believe she came in today."

He put his hands over his face and then looked back at her. "Is she okay?"

"Some kind of family emergency. I think? I'm not sure. Did you try calling her?"

"Never mind." Zachary stormed out of the building and pulled out his phone, tempted to text again. Obviously, if Jasmine could get back to him, she would. If her phone had burned up, then she wasn't getting the texts, anyway. It was pointless to keep texting. He would either annoy her or send them nowhere.

His best bet was to go to the high school—although the question was which one. The new one that had just been built or the old one? They were miles apart and he'd left his car back at home, so he'd have to walk unless he wanted to go home first.

The old high school was almost in between the gym and his parents' house, so if Jasmine wasn't there, he could swing by to get his car and go to the other school.

While he walked, he searched for more articles on the fire, trying to find out if anyone had been injured. The first one hadn't mentioned anything beyond the temporary shelter.

About a block from the high school, his phone beeped. He had a text.

Zachary closed the browser app and went to his text messages.

I'm so sorry. I didn't hear my phone and I didn't realize how late it was. I won't be able to make it for lunch.

Relief swept through him. At least she was well enough to text him. *Are you okay?*

Yeah. Just at the hospital.

What? His heart nearly stopped beating.

I'm visiting my mom. Sorry. I'm not a patient.

Zachary leaned against a nearby pole, trying to catch his breath.

When you get a chance, you'll have to tell me everything. I was worried you were in the fire.

I was, but I'm fine. Can I call you when I leave here?

Yeah. Let me know what I can do.

Thanks, Zachary. Really sorry about lunch.

Don't worry about it.

Zachary took a minute to steady his breathing. She was okay at least, and probably had an interesting story to tell. Once he'd recovered, he stopped at a coffee stand and used his last five dollar bill to order an iced mocha for the walk home. The sun beat down on him and thinking that Jasmine had been hurt and in the hospital had made his mouth go dry.

He finished the drink before he'd made it a block,

dumped the cup into a garbage can, and went back home. The house was quiet. He wanted to talk to someone to get everything off his chest, but it wasn't meant to be.

Instead, he went to his room and turned on his laptop. With the wild emotions racing through him, it would be the perfect time to write. He had a scene coming up where Damion was going to be chased by mobsters, and writing about that would help him to release everything he felt.

Zachary made himself comfortable on his bed and started typing as fast as his fingers would go. He made a lot of spelling errors, but he didn't bother to stop and fix anything. He was in the flow, and besides, that was what spell-check was for.

By the time he stopped typing, he felt a lot better about everything—and he had three new chapters. He looked it over and realized that was the most he'd ever typed in one day. Checking the time, he realized he'd managed to do that in just under three hours. The most and the fastest in one day.

He got up and went to the living room, surprised to find his parents and Rafael playing cards.

"When did you guys get here?" Zachary asked.

"We've been here a while," Rafael said, "but when Mom heard you typing a million words a minute, she said we needed to let you be."

Zachary chuckled. "It wasn't that fast."

"Sounded like you were going to set your keyboard on fire," said his mom.

"Well, I did beat my previous record."

"Finally found your muse?" asked his dad.

"There's no such thing as a muse."

"I wouldn't know." He turned back to the cards in his hand and then placed one on the table. "Rafael, your turn."

Zachary sat down and watched them play a few rounds, checking his phone every so often.

"Expecting a call?" asked his mom.

"Or are we boring you?" Rafael joked.

"Just hoping to hear from someone."

"Who?" asked his dad.

There was no such thing as privacy when it came to his family. "I made friends with one of the people living in the building where that fire was."

His mom looked up at him with concern in her eyes. "Is he okay?"

Zachary felt heat creep into his cheeks. "Yeah. She's fine."

Six eyes focused on him.

"She?" asked his mom, looking excited. Her dream was for all the Hunter boys to get married and have a bunch of children running around.

"I thought you were going to take a break after Monica," Rafael said, discarding half of his hand onto the table. "Your turn, Mom."

"First, I want to hear more about this girl Zachary likes."

He looked away. "I didn't say I liked her—I just said we're friends."

"You're blushing," Rafael said, grinning. "What's her name? Is she a local? Does she—?"

"What about your girlfriend?" Zachary asked, trying to turn the focus off himself.

Rafael frowned. "If you don't want to talk about the girl, just say so. You don't need to bring up my love life."

"What happened?" Zachary asked, taken aback by his brother's sudden change in mood.

"It didn't work out. That's all."

"Why not?" asked their mom.

Rafael glared at Zachary, and then turned to his mom. "I'm not ready to talk about it. It just didn't work out. Can you guys let it be?"

She reached over and patted his arm. "Sure, but know you can always talk to us."

"I know." He shot another look at Zachary.

"Anyone want a snack?" Zachary asked, squirming. "I can grab something."

"Sure," said his dad. "I could use something to drink."

"Me, too," said his mom. "Rafael?"

"No. I'm fine." He kept his attention on his cards.

"You sure?" Zachary asked.

Rafael shot him an irritated look. "Yes."

"Okay." Zachary went into the kitchen and got some chips, putting them into a bowl, and then he got drinks for his parents. He balanced them all and went back into the living room. He set the stuff around them and the game, and then checked his phone again. Still, no more texts. "I'm going outside for some air."

He went outside and leaned against the house, feeling a headache coming on. Pressure built all around his head, centering on his forehead and sinuses. It was amazing the stress family could bring at times. He understood Rafael not wanting to talk about his breakup, but at the same time, Zachary himself didn't feel like opening up about Jasmine yet, either.

A little while later, he heard the front door open and then shut.

"What was that about?" came a familiar voice.

Rafael appeared in front of him, arms folded. His slicked back hair didn't move in the breeze that had picked up over the last few minutes, but his silk shirt blew around.

"I don't want to talk about her," Zachary said. "It's too soon to say anything. I'm just getting to know her."

"So, you thought I wanted to talk about my breakup with Kristine?" Rafael narrowed his eyes.

"You seemed to want to talk about relationships. And I didn't know you broke up. I'm sorry. Really."

"Look. If you don't want to talk about the girl, just

say so. Don't bring me into it." He stepped closer, still glaring at Zachary.

"Back off, Raf."

Rafael stepped closer. "I said don't do it again. I'm not talking about what happened. Maybe I never will— I don't care how tight we are—or used to be, at least."

"Whatever," Zachary said. "Just give me some space."

"I want to make sure you understand."

Zachary felt anger building. "Got it. Now get outta my face."

Rafael took a couple steps back. "Thank you. I know you guys are family and would do anything for me—I'd do anything for all of you—but this... this is different, and I don't want to talk about Kristine. And it's not just a matter of needing to wait to talk about it. I don't know if I'll ever be able to discuss it."

Zachary's anger dissipated. "Sounds like it was really rough, whatever it was. Sorry it happened. I'm sure you didn't deserve it."

"No, I didn't." He leaned against the house next to Zachary. "I wish I could say I came here out of altruistic love from my heart, but it isn't the case. My entire life imploded on me—all within about a week. It's too much, and I want to forget everything that happened in LA. Once I buy my house, I'm shipping everything up and never going back again."

"Well, if you need any help getting settled in or anything, let me know. We used to be close, and like you said, we're family. I'd do anything for you, too."

Rafael looked at him. "Thanks, Zachary."

Zachary turned to look at him and froze. His brother had tears shining in his eyes—and Zachary had never once seen that side of Rafael. Not in all their years.

Thirteen

～

JASMINE STARED AT THE CLOCK on the wall in the hospital cafeteria. She'd been at the hospital all day, waiting for her mom to wake. She'd been out from some pain medication, but they were supposed to reduce the dose to see how she did with it. That meant she would wake up, and she might even be awake by now.

Sighing, Jasmine finished the salad languishing front of her and then the juice. If she gave it a little more time, her mom would hopefully be awake enough to have a conversation. She just had to give the hospital staff time to do their thing first.

They were borderline ready to send her to the burn unit, but needed to talk to her about her pain levels. The nurses had spoken to Jasmine at length about the benefits of the burn unit, but it was reserved for the most severe burns. Jasmine's mom would have scars for the rest of her life once her skin healed, but they didn't think specialized care was necessary—unless she was in more pain than they thought, and that was impossible to know with her sleeping and on meds.

Jasmine pretended to be the caring, loving daughter but really, she thought her mom had it coming. She's been smoking while drinking and then fell asleep, ruining the lives of easily more than a hundred people. And it wasn't even the first time this had happened.

She crinkled up the juice box and put it on the tray before throwing all the garbage away. On her way out of the cafeteria, she passed a doctor and noticed his tag said Dr. Hunter. Jasmine did a double take at his tag.

"Can I help you?" asked the tall, handsome doctor.

Embarrassed, Jasmine shook her head. "I know someone named Hunter, and your tag caught my attention. Sorry to bother you."

He smiled, putting her at ease. "I'm related to most of the Hunters in the area. Who do you know?"

Heat crept into her cheeks. "His name is Zachary."

The doctor smiled wider. "Ah, my younger brother and work out buddy."

"So, you're the one he's been working out with," Jasmine said, forgetting about her mom for a minute. She smiled.

"Are you the one he's had some meals with?" The doctor appeared curious.

She nodded. "My name is Jasmine."

"Brayden." He held out his hand, and they shook. "Nice to meet you, Jasmine. Hopefully, I'll see you around."

"I hope so, too."

Brayden tilted his head and then joined some other doctors, discussing medical stuff.

Jasmine's heart picked up speed thinking about Zachary. Did he and Brayden talk about her when they worked out?

She pulled out her phone from her pocket and texted him.

Hopefully I won't be much longer here. Are you available to meet when I'm done?

Name the time and place, and I'll be there.

Jasmine grinned. *Perfect. I'll let you know when I'm ready.*

I can't wait.

Butterflies danced in her stomach. He couldn't wait to see her. She couldn't wait to see him, either. In fact, she was tempted to skip seeing her mom and just meet Zachary. He was by far the more pleasant company of the two.

But she really needed to talk to her mom, and from the sounds of it, there would be less privacy in the burn unit—if her mom was admitted there—to say what needed to be said. Her mood souring, Jasmine made her way to her mom's room and found her sitting up, watching TV. She came in, not saying anything and then sat on the chair closest to the door. Farthest from her mom.

Jasmine cleared her throat. "You're awake."

Her mom turned to her. "Never could get anything by you."

Jasmine bit her tongue. "How's your arm feel?"

"Not half as bad as it looks."

Because of the meds, but Jasmine wasn't going to say that.

"Are they going to move you to the burn unit?" Jasmine asked.

"Doesn't sound like it. Someone from there just left, and after ripping the bandages off, gave directions to the doctors here."

Jasmine forced a smile. "That's certainly good news. When are they supposed to send you back home?"

"Not soon enough. They won't let me smoke or drink."

"You still want to smoke? After causing another fire?" Jasmine's voice was shrill.

"It would sure help this damn headache." Her mom rubbed her temple with her good arm.

"They have you on painkillers. It would be a lot worse without them."

"Guess we know what my first purchases is going to be when I get out of here."

Jasmine shook her head. Her time would have been much better spent with Zachary.

"Don't you judge me, girl," her mom snapped, her voice especially raspy.

"Judge you?" Jasmine exclaimed. "I don't have to. Your life speaks for itself."

They stared each other down.

Jasmine finally spoke. "Why did you show up at my place? I never even got the chance to find out what's going on—because you set it on fire and put a ton of people out with nowhere to stay."

Her mom narrowed her eyes. "I can't live with your dad anymore. I just can't do it."

"Then get your own trailer." Jasmine folded her arms.

"With what money?" demanded her mom.

"You're a grown woman," Jasmine said. "I'm sure you can figure it out."

"I don't got a job."

"Then get one." Jasmine narrowed her eyes.

They stared at each other for a minute before her mom spoke. "I don't have the benefits you do, Jas. You're young and energetic. No one wants to hire an old lady."

Jasmine shook her head. "You know what? If you stopped drinking and smoking, I bet you'd take ten years off your face."

Her mom scowled. "You don't know anything."

"I know plenty. More than you. Ever since I left home, I've been taking care of myself and having a great time. Until you showed up, that is. Now my life is a mess again. So, thanks for that. At least I can count on you for something."

"You need to help me get on my feet."

Jasmine laughed bitterly. "No, I don't."

"Your brother would have."

Anger shot through Jasmine. She narrowed her eyes. "Don't ever bring up Carter in my presence again. He followed in your footsteps, and look what happened." Hot, angry tears stung her eyes. "He was smart. Remember that? They put him in the program for the exceptionally bright. You probably don't remember, because neither you nor Dad cared. He had that ceremony, remember? Oh, wait. You wouldn't—because I was the only one who went."

"Do you think now's the time to bring up my mistakes?" asked her mom.

"It seems as good a time as any," Jasmine snapped. "You showed up at my condo and burned it down. I think I have the right to talk about whatever I want."

"Why don't you just leave?" her mom asked. "You're not helping me none."

"Facing your demons is the best thing you could do. Maybe it will wake you up enough to stop being so destructive. Now you have a physical reminder."

Her mom touched the fresh bandages. "I can wear long sleeves. Then I can pretend it doesn't exist." She stuck her nose in the air.

"What good is that going to do? You need to sober up and get a job. That's the only way you'll get away from Dad. You always say you want away from him, but you don't do anything about it. You never have. Not in the twenty-six years I've known you."

"I did, actually."

Jasmine raised an eyebrow.

"I walked out, not that he noticed. Then I found you, and you didn't make that easy, but I did. I'm taking steps to change things."

"You need to try harder," Jasmine said. "If you'll go to rehab, I'll help you. Only then. Rehab. And it goes against my better judgment, but if you're serious and willing to put in the hard work, I'll see what I can do."

"Rehab?" her mom exclaimed. "Are you serious?"

"Yes. And you have to succeed." Jasmine sat taller and stared into her mom's yellowish eyes.

"Do you know how long I've lived like this? My body couldn't even survive without alcohol and tobacco. I can't even think straight right now with the pains ravaging my head."

"You know what?" Jasmine asked. "That's your body trying to get rid of all the toxins you've put in for all those years. It *wants* to be healthy, but you won't let it."

Her mom closed her eyes. "My arms hurts. I'm going back to sleep."

"You just woke up." Jasmine narrowed her eyes.

"I don't want to be awake."

Jasmine shook her head. "Since you came out here to see me, I'm going to be back. I'll be here every day. Maybe more than once a day. Think about what I said. It's either rehab or going back to Dad. Think about that for a while."

Her mom groaned, but didn't open her eyes.

Jasmine stormed out of the room. She wanted to scream—a typical response after spending time with her mom. Instead, she stopped at the nurses' station.

"Any chance of having my mom sent to a drug rehab center after she's released?" she asked the nurse.

"Is the patient addicted to drugs?"

"The easier question to answer is which ones isn't she addicted to." Jasmine stared at the nurse.

"Which room is the patient in?"

Jasmine told her.

"Okay. I'll leave a message for the floor's social worker. Her job is to be an advocate for all the patients. I'll need your number because she's going to want to talk to you."

"Gladly." Jasmine wrote the number down and then finally made her way out of the hospital. She'd been there far too long and had wasted a day off work. With as long as her mom had been unconscious, she could have taught her classes and then come over. Not only that, but she could have had her lunch date with Zachary.

What a waste.

When she got outside, Jasmine realized she was without a car. Kate had insisted on driving her, and now she was stuck. She could either call Kate and then wait—and go stir-crazy—or she could call for a cab. That would probably be a lot quicker.

She went inside where it was cooler. It was comfortable and she realized how much she just wanted to relax. She hadn't slept well on the cot, and then dealing with her mom all day, even when she was unconscious, had been too much. All she wanted was to sit and read Zachary's book. She'd wanted to finish the night before, but that had been a bust. No more tablet, but at least she had an app on her phone.

Maybe waiting for Kate to return wasn't such as bad idea. Even if Kate couldn't get there for another hour, that would be an hour Jasmine could sit by herself and get lost in the world Zachary had created. She was dying to know what happened to Damion, anyway.

She sat down in a plush chair near a water fountain. She watched the water for a few minutes, trying to relax. It helped somewhat. Then she pulled her phone out and texted Kate just to be sure.

> *Are you able to pick me up or should I call a cab?*
>
> *I'm teaching a class now. It's just about to start. How long can you wait?*
>
> *Doesn't matter. I'm in no hurry.*

How's your mom?

Moody, but awake.

If you don't mind hanging out with her, I can get you.

Okay.

See you in a couple hours.

Thanks.

No way was Jasmine going back to visit with her mom. She'd settle down with the book and lose herself in a thrilling, imaginary world. Nothing else sounded better—with the only exception being to see Zachary, but she couldn't ask him to drive all that way. It would be over an hour round trip. It had taken them nearly forty minutes just to get to the hospital that morning.

Just as Jasmine had settled into the story, she heard her name. Looking up, she saw Zachary's brother standing near her.

"Hi… Brandon, was it?" she asked.

He smiled. "Close. Brayden."

"Right, Brayden. Sorry."

"No worries. Is everything okay?" he asked.

"Yeah. I'm just waiting for my ride back home… uh, to Kittle Falls." She had no home.

Brayden sat in the chair next to her. "What brings you to the hospital?"

"Just my mom." She wasn't going to admit to being related to the person who had caused the fire.

"Is she all right?"

STACY CLAFLIN

"She will be."

He nodded. "That's good. I'm actually headed back to Kittle Falls. If you want to ride with me, I'd be more than happy to drop you off wherever you need to go. Or if you don't want to ride with a stranger, I understand. But I can take you to my parents' house. I happen to know that's where Zachary is right now." Brayden smiled.

Jasmine's heart nearly leaped into her throat. "You don't mind?"

"Not at all. Like I said, I'm headed that way now."

"Hold on." Jasmine pulled out her phone and sent Kate a text.

Never mind. I found another ride.

Fourteen

~

ZACHARY SNATCHED THE BASKETBALL FROM Rafael and shot it into the hoop, making a perfect shot. "Take that."

Rafael ran over to where the ball bounced, grabbed it, and jumped up, making a slam dunk. "Take that, little brother."

"Always with the pecking order." Zachary shook his head and pointed to the right. "What's that?"

"What?" Rafael asked.

Laughing, Zachary grabbed the ball, stepped back, and made another perfect shot.

"Seriously?" Rafael asked. "That's such a snotty, little brother move."

"But you fell for it." Zachary laughed again.

Rafael cracked a smile. "Hope you enjoyed it because that's the last time."

A car pulled into the driveway. Zachary and Rafael moved out of the way, with Rafael hanging onto the ball. He shot Zachary a look that only an older brother could get away with. It was crazy how playing ball with his brother could reduce them both to acting like competitive teens in a matter of minutes.

Zachary looked as the Mercedes with tinted windows pulled into the driveway. It was only Brayden—and he would likely want to play on Rafael's side. Those two had always sided together when playing hoops—ever since they were all kids. Zachary grabbed the ball, but this time Rafael had a tight hold on it, refusing to let go.

They both tugged and pulled, until they ended up on the grass, rolling around to gain control of the ball. Finally, Zachary pulled it out of Rafael's grip, but then his brother pushed his face into the dirt, getting it in his eyes.

Not to be overtaken that easily, Zachary held the ball closer and stood, running to the other end of the yard. Rafael, dressed perfectly, now ran after him covered in soil and grass. Zachary laughed at the sight, but then stopped cold when Jasmine stepped out of Brayden's car.

He thought he was imagining her—until she waved.

Rafael wasted no time, taking advantage of Zachary's distraction. He snatched the ball from his hands, and ran toward the hoop.

Not in front of Jasmine.

Zachary ran after his brother, knocking him to the ground from behind.

"What gives?" Rafael grunted.

"I need to make that shot." Zachary grabbed the ball and jumped up, running toward the hoop. He felt his brother's arms wrap around his waist. Zachary focused on the hoop. It was pretty far away, but he was a decent shot. He could do this—he had to with Jasmine watching.

He held the ball close, focused on the hoop, and threw it, aiming for the middle. It sailed through the air, as if in slow motion. It hit the rim and rolled around it, teetering toward the outside, and then moving toward the inside. It went around, moving back and forth between falling through the hoop and outside of it.

He held his breath as he watched, feeling his manhood on the line. There was no way he was going to let his brother get the best of him in front of Jasmine.

The ball seemed to go around in circles forever before finally tipping inward and falling through the hoop.

"Yes!" Zachary cheered, clenching his fists close to him.

Rafael shot him a dirty look, but said, "Nice shot."

Jasmine came over. "I agree. You have some good moves." She dusted some dirt off his arm.

Rafael raised an eyebrow at Zachary as if starting to understand.

Zachary turned to Jasmine. "This is my brother, Rafael. Rafael, Jasmine."

"Nice to meet you," Jasmine said, smiling.

"Likewise." They shook hands.

"How many brothers do you have?" Jasmine asked, glancing between the three present Hunter brothers.

"There are five of us," Zachary said. "I take it you've met Brayden. I didn't know he was bringing you over here." He shot Brayden a questioning expression.

Brayden shrugged and mouthed, "Sorry."

Zachary shook his head. "Yeah, right."

"We ran into each other at the hospital," Jasmine said, seemingly oblivious to Zachary's irritation. "I saw his tag and asked if you two were related. I thought it was a small world, but if there are five of you, I suppose not."

"If you've spent much time here in town," Rafael said, "you've probably run into the other two without knowing it."

"More than likely," Brayden agreed. "Well, I need to get over to the clinic and approve some carpeting. It won't be much longer now." His face lit up.

"Have fun," Zachary said, his mood lifting. "We'll talk later."

Brayden laughed. "I'm sure we will. Bye, Jasmine."

She waved. "Thanks for the ride."

"Anytime." Brayden got back into his car and drove away.

"I didn't know you were coming over," Zachary said, "or I would have cleaned up." He brushed some dirt away from his eyes.

Jasmine smiled. "I enjoyed watching you two wrestle. It reminded me of my brother."

"Oh?" Zachary asked. "So you know how annoying they can be." He glanced over at Rafael.

Rafael shoved him. "You know it. I'm going inside to get cleaned up. I'm not sure this shirt is salvageable."

"Maybe you shouldn't wear designer threads when shooting hoops," Zachary teased.

"I can always design more. Besides, this shirt is from last year." He shrugged.

"You *designed* that?" Jasmine asked, appearing impressed.

"He runs a small design—"

"Ran," Rafael corrected. "I'm starting over up here. There's an empty retail space next to the bridal shop where I'm going to sell my clothes."

"Wow," Jasmine said. "Is your whole family so successful? A novelist, a doctor, and a fashion designer."

"We also have a tattoo artist and a shop owner," Rafael said.

"Owner?" Zachary asked.

"Oops. I wasn't supposed to say anything," Rafael said. "You can't tell anyone. Jake and our parents are going to tell everyone at dinner tonight. Jake's buying the Hunter Family Store from them. Anyway, catch you guys later." He went inside.

She stepped closer to Zachary, but he backed up. "You probably don't want to get too close. If I had any idea you were on your way over, I would have washed up."

Jasmine stepped closer. "I don't mind. Like I said, you reminded me of my brother. It was nice to think about good memories for a change."

"Oh?" he asked with heightened awareness to how close she stood while he was covered in dirt, grass stains, and perspiration.

She shook her head. "I don't really have many good memories with him, unfortunately."

"You guys can always make new memories. I've found that as we get older, my brothers and I have gotten closer. Even if we do wrestle from time to time." He smiled.

Jasmine gave him a weak smile. "Carter and I can't make any new memories."

"No?" Zachary asked.

Sadness covered her face. "He's gone."

"Oh," Zachary said, his joy deflated. "I know how that feels."

She gazed at him, her face curious.

"We used to have a sister."

Jasmine's eyes widened. "I'm so sorry."

Zachary nodded and indicated toward a bench swing under a tree not far away. "Want to sit?"

She nodded, and then they walked over and sat. He took her hand and rubbed her palm. "Sounds like we've both had our share of heartache," she said.

"Unfortunately. What happened with your brother? If you want to talk about it."

Jasmine sighed, a tear rolling down her face. "It was a car accident a long time ago. He never even got to graduate high school, and he would've been the first in our entire family to not only graduate, but with honors."

"No one in your family graduated high school?" Zachary asked, confused. Had she not? Not that he would have liked her any less, it was just surprising.

Her cheeks turned pink. "Not until I did. Carter and I didn't exactly come from a line of high achievers."

"Sounds like you two are real heroes. I imagine it would be hard to break out of a mold like that."

Jasmine shrugged. "He was born with natural talent, and I just wanted to get away from everything. So I focused on dance. It pretty much saved me." She looked away. "That probably sounds stupid."

Zachary slid his fingers through hers and squeezed. "Not even close. It was fairly easy to succeed in my family—it was practically expected. With Brayden leading the way, and five competitive boys...." He frowned. "Now I'm the one who probably sounds dumb."

She stared at him, her eyes wide. "Not at all. I wish I could've grown up in a home like that." Her face clouded over.

He wanted to ask what her childhood had been like,

but didn't want to push. If she wanted to talk about it, she would. He'd already managed to tick off his brother, he didn't want to add Jasmine to that list.

"What happened with your sister?" she asked.

"Cancer." Zachary couldn't bring himself to say more than that.

Jasmine nodded. "That sucks." She scooted closer and leaned her head against his shoulder.

He was tempted to scoot away, knowing how dirty he was, but he didn't. They were sharing a moment, and if she didn't care, then neither did he. At least he didn't stink. The deodorant was doing its job.

"Did you ever feel like instead of just being you, you became just the brother of that dead kid?" she asked, frowning.

"For a little while, I suppose. But then I moved to New York and became just another face in the crowd."

Jasmine scooted even closer and their bare legs pressed against each other. Zachary took a deep breath and tried to focus on her heartache instead. He wrapped his free arm around her and rubbed her shoulder.

"After he died," Jasmine whispered, "everyone treated me differently. Even my best friends. It was like no one knew how to act toward me. Like I would break or something? Yeah, I was heartbroken, but it wasn't like I was a different person, you know. I was still me, just without my big brother."

Zachary leaned his head on top of hers. "It wasn't

quite like that for me, but I know what you mean. People did look at me differently for a while. But then again, I suppose I was used to stares. The only family in town with six kids. When people see me, if they don't know me personally, they just see one of the Hunter siblings. And with that, yes, the loss of Sophia."

Jasmine seemed to relax in his arms. "It's nice to meet someone who understands."

"I wish neither of us had to."

They sat in silence for a while until his mom came out with a tray holding a pitcher and two glasses. She set it next to Zachary. "I thought you two might be thirsty." She extended her hand toward Jasmine. "I'm Dawn, Zachary's mother."

Jasmine took her hand and shook it. "Jasmine. It's a pleasure to meet you, Mrs. Hunter. You have very nice sons. At least the three I've met."

"You should stay for dinner, and then you can meet the others, and Tiffany and Lana, too."

"That sounds wonderful," Jasmine said. "I'd like that, thank you."

"Great. I'll let you two be." She walked away.

"Your whole family seems so nice," Jasmine said.

"Mostly." Zachary shrugged. They all had their flaws like any other family. "So, what was your brother like?"

"He was a good guy," she said. "He just got caught up in some stuff he shouldn't have. I wish he would've made more friends with the smart kids in his honors classes, but he didn't." She let a long, slow breath. "I like to think if he knew how things would play out, he would've made better choices."

"I don't mean to pry, but did he cause the accident?" Zachary asked.

She nodded, her hair tickling his face. "He was drunk—way over the legal limit. Unfortunately, my parents weren't exactly sober that night, so I had to drive them down to…." She paused, shaking next to him.

Zachary squeezed her. "It's okay. You don't have to talk about it."

Jasmine dissolved into tears. She pressed her face against his chest, shaking even harder, soaking his shirt with her tears. He ran his hands over her hair and then kissed the top of her head, trying to be gentle enough that she wouldn't notice. She wrapped her arms around him, still crying.

Fifteen

~

JASMINE GASPED FOR AIR, EXHAUSTED from sobbing. She had cried harder than she ever had. Even harder than when Carter had passed. Then, there had been no time to mourn. After he'd died, she'd been forced to take care of her parents, cleaning up after them. After the funeral, the ash trays had filled up faster than ever before and empty bottles littered the floor in every room of the house.

After about a month, her mom had caused the first house fire. Once they settled into a new trailer, Jasmine counted down the days until her graduation. She started her junior year working, cleaning up after her parents, dealing with the stares of classmates, and somehow getting her homework done in between everything else.

It felt good to cry, even though it was long overdue. She hadn't even let herself think about Carter since graduation until her mom showed up.

Jasmine glanced up at Zachary and then noticed out of the corner of her eye that her makeup was smeared all over his light blue shirt. Her black mascara, eyeliner, and brown eyeshadow had left a huge smear on the chest of his shirt.

"Sorry about your shirt," she said, her voice wavering.

He looked down. "It's nothing. I'm more concerned about you." He wiped underneath her eye, his finger lingering on her face.

Jasmine stared into his eyes, her pulse racing at his touch. She felt raw and exposed, but yet safe at the same time. That was something she wasn't used to feeling—she'd never opened up to anyone like that. She kept everyone at a distance on purpose.

The last thing she wanted was to risk wounding anyone the way she'd been. She wasn't so much worried about being hurt. That was something she knew she could deal with—she'd had plenty of practice.

Jasmine was aware of Zachary's finger still on her face. He slid it down slightly until it rested underneath her chin. Suddenly, she wanted him to kiss her.

They continued to stare into each other's eyes, the tension between them thickening by the moment. She was frozen by her emotions, but tried to beg him with her eyes to press his lips against hers. Had she not been so shaken up, she would have moved toward him.

He put pressure on her chin with his finger, brought her face closer to him while he moved his near her. He closed his eyes, and butterflies danced—no, stomped and screamed—in her stomach. His lips brushed against hers and then he pressed firmly. His hand moved from her hair to the small of her back, pushing her closer to him.

Jasmine breathed in deeply, closing her eyes. He smelled of sandalwood and grass, an odd mixture, but surprisingly pleasant. She pressed her lips against his. They were soft and warm, making her feel even safer than she had a moment ago when she had been staring into his eyes.

Zachary pulled back and Jasmine opened her eyes, meeting his gaze. She had never experienced such a kiss. He'd kept it sweet, not opening his mouth, but somehow managed to fill it with passion. She stared at him, wanting more but knowing it would have to wait.

He ran his fingertips along her cheeks, not saying a word. It tickled her skin slightly, but she liked it. She felt a connection so deep she'd never felt that close to anyone before. It was as though she stared directly into his soul.

Zachary cleared his throat. "Do you want some of that lemonade?"

She nodded, unable to find her voice.

He turned around and picked up a glass and poured the drink in. He handed it to her before pouring his own. Jasmine took a sip, surprised at how tasty it was. It was the perfect mixture of sweet and sour, refreshing her from the heat.

They sat in silence, sipping the lemonade until the pitcher emptied. Zachary took her glass and put it on the tray, and then sat back, putting his arm around her again. She snuggled closer, taking in his rugged scent again.

Birds flew through the air, darting down toward the ground and then flying circles around the yard before landing in a bird bath and splashing around.

Jasmine wanted to say something, but wasn't sure what. Especially after the sobbing, ruining his shirt, and especially the kiss. Wow. What was left say? She felt emptied—but in a good way.

"Have you visited Carter's grave?" Zachary asked.

"Not in a long time," Jasmine admitted. "I haven't been back home in years."

"At least you have that excuse."

"You haven't visited your sister's?" she asked.

He shook his head. "Not since the funeral, actually. I just can't bring myself to. I'm afraid it will bring everything back, and I'm not sure I want to deal with it all over again. Though, now I'm having second thoughts."

Jasmine took his hand. "If you want me to go with you, I will. Or if you want to go alone, do that. But it might be easier with the company."

Zachary squeezed her hand. "It would be nice to go with you. If I went with one of my brothers...." He sighed. "I'm not sure I could do that. It might just be too much."

Her heart swelled at his vulnerability. It couldn't be easy to admit his fears. "I know what you mean. There's no way I could visit Carter with my parents."

"Would you mind going now?" he asked, sitting taller.

"Now?" she asked.

"Before I chicken out."

"You're not a chicken."

Zachary smiled. "I might be, but the only way to prove you right is if we go immediately."

"We'd better go, then. Do you want to change your shirt?" she asked, feeling guilty for smearing her makeup all over it.

"And give me time to talk myself out of it? No. I need to do this. Now." He rose, helped her up, and studied her face. "You're beautiful, you know that?"

Jasmine's cheeks burned and she looked away. "No, I'm not."

Zachary placed his finger underneath her chin and turned it, pulling some of her hair behind her ear. "You are. You're gorgeous, and your heart is even more so."

Her heart pounded in her chest, threatening to break through her ribs. She wasn't used to anyone saying things like that. Even the few boyfriends she'd had over the years never said anything like that. Jasmine had a tendency to pick guys that ended up like her family. How had she managed to find Zachary? He was perfect—handsome, well built, imaginative, and kind-hearted.

Hopefully, she wouldn't do anything stupid to lose him.

"You're even prettier when you blush," he said, staring into her eyes.

She shook her head.

He pulled her close and kissed her nose. "I'm going to keep telling you how beautiful you are until you believe it."

"That's going to take a long time." Jasmine covered her mouth. She hasn't meant to say that aloud.

Zachary stepped back and stared deeper into her eyes, his expression melting her insides.

"Then I'll keep telling you for years if I have to. The day you believe it, I'll stop." He brushed his finger across her cheek.

She opened her mouth to speak, but he put a finger to her lips.

"I hope you believe it. You really are beautiful."

Jasmine took his hand from her lips and laced her fingers through his. "Let's get going before it gets too close to dinnertime. We're supposed to eat with your family, remember."

"We should probably drive, in that case," he said. "I hope you don't mind that my car isn't as nice as Brayden's."

"Neither is mine."

"It's still probably better than mine," he said. "I had to trade down big time in the Big Apple."

She shrugged. "It takes more than a car to impress me, and you've already done that."

"I have?" he asked, looking genuinely surprised.

"Most definitely."

"Let's hope my car doesn't ruin that." He laughed nervously.

"I can't see that happening."

Zachary raised her hand and kissed the back of it. Then he led her across the street to an old car with rusty rims and a number of dents. He let go of her hand and unlocked the passenger door with a key.

"Remote locks are for the birds," he joked and then gestured for her to get in.

"This isn't so bad," Jasmine said, sitting down. A spring dug into her back, but she smiled, ignoring it.

He got in and dug underneath the seat, pulling out a clear CD box with a recordable disc inside. It had bubbly, cursive writing with hearts over the I's.

"What's that?" Jasmine asked.

"It's all of Sophia's favorite songs. She left this in my old car the last time I gave her a ride. I think I was taking her to a school dance. She and her friends were meeting without guys because one of them had just been dumped." He smiled, looking lost in thought. "She had a boyfriend who she adored, but her friends were so close they all ditched their guys to support the dumped friend."

"Aw, that's sweet." Jasmine smiled. "It sounds like she was a great girl."

"That she was." Tears shone in his eyes. "Mind if we listen? I don't even remember what's on there. Though I've kept it in here, I haven't been able to listen to it. Now I finally feel ready."

Jasmine's heart swelled even more than it already had. If she wasn't careful, she'd end up falling in love— and Zachary was quickly winning her over with his kindness and vulnerability. She'd never met anyone like him. He was someone she could see herself falling for, and hard.

She watched him slide the CD into the player and couldn't help admiring him. He handled the disc with such care she could see even further how much his sister still meant to him.

Zachary glanced over at her, meeting her gaze. Tears shone in his eyes as a sweet love song from about four or five years earlier played. "I remember her dancing through the house to this. One time she even used a loaf of French bread as a microphone." He laughed, though tears ran down his face.

Jasmine leaned over and wiped some of his tears away. He held onto her hand and pressed it against his chest so that she could feel his heart pounding against her palm.

"Thank you for everything," he whispered.

"I haven't done anything."

"You've done more than you know." He blinked, spilling out more tears.

Jasmine leaned across to his seat and, heart pounding loud enough for him to hear, she kissed the tears away. Even the ones sticking to his lashes. He closed his eyes, squeezing her hand. She kissed along the path of tears and then sat back, watching him.

A new song played. This one was upbeat, and from about the same time period.

Zachary opened his eyes. "She used to belt this one out all over the place. Even in the shower." He shook his head, smiling. "Her voice carried so that no matter where you were in the house, you could hear her singing."

Jasmine leaned against him and they listened to the song together. When a new one started, she asked, "Do you want me to drive?"

"I... well... I'm not sure."

She leaned back in her seat, ignoring the sharp spring. "It's not like I'm going to make it any worse than it already is," she teased.

He smiled that beautiful smile of his, another tear spilling onto his face. "That's not what I meant."

Sixteen

~

ZACHARY CLIMBED OUT OF THE passenger seat of his own car, clutching the bouquet of flowers that Jasmine had picked out and purchased. He shook just thinking about visiting Sophia's grave. He hadn't even seen the tombstone in person. Jake had shown him pictures shortly after it had been erected.

He locked the car and then followed the path toward where his sister rested. The permanence of her death hit him at that moment. Obviously, he knew she was gone and that he would never see her again, but going back to where they had laid her a few years ago… it was like a smack to his face.

His knees gave out, but Jasmine must have been right next to him—he hadn't even noticed—because suddenly her arms went around his waist.

"Easy there," she said. "I'm here for you, and if you want privacy, then I'll give you that, too."

His voice caught in his throat, but he managed to find it. "I want you there."

"I have all day." She tightened her grip around his waist, helping him walk.

Zachary's stomach twisted in knots and he felt like he would lose his lunch. That was all he needed, for Jasmine to witness that. He let go of the flowers with one hand and wrapped that arm around her for support, in more ways than one.

They came to an intersecting path.

"Which way do we go?" Jasmine asked.

Zachary looked around, trying to remember. It had been three years, but he recognized the path down to the left. It had a statue of a crying angel. They followed the path. Nearly everything was exactly as he remembered back on the worst day of his life. No one should have to bury their baby sister, ever.

He slowed when they reached a row of tombstones that seemed familiar. There had only been a few when he'd been there, but now not only was the row filled out, but many more were as well. Had that many people in Kittle Falls died over the last three years?

"This row?" Jasmine asked.

Zachary took a deep breath and swallowed. He looked down, remembering standing there with his family and so many of Sophia's friends.

"Must be that one," Jasmine said.

He saw the one she meant. There was one with a teddy bear, framed pictures, dried flowers, and even some envelopes. "Popular even in death." Zachary's voice cracked.

Jasmine moved her arm up to his shoulders and squeezed. "Are you ready?"

His body felt cold despite the heat of the day and Jasmine's warm embrace. He shivered, not wanting to face it—and the fact that he'd mostly been pretending that Sophia was away, only traveling somewhere. If only that were the case. He shivered.

"Come on," Jasmine said, taking a step.

"I can see it from here."

"Let's take a look at the inscription," said Jasmine.

Zachary had the sudden urge to stomp his foot and say that he refused to look. It would be easier to continue living in an imaginary world where his sister was in Paris or some other place she'd dreamed of going, but would never have the chance to visit. He swallowed, unable to ignore the lump in his throat.

He took one step, and then another. All too soon, they stood in front of the grave where his sister had been for the last three years. Zachary dropped to his knees, his vision blurring with more tears. He blinked them away, forcing himself to admire at the stone. It sparkled like new, even more than the others around it.

Someone had been cleaning it—but who?

Finally, he read the inscription: *Sophia Anastasia Hunter, beloved daughter and sister.* The dates of her life followed, and an angel was sketched off to the side. It was both beautiful and crushing.

"I'm so sorry, Sophia," Zachary whispered, barely audible to his own ears. "I didn't visit because... because... I have no excuse aside from being scared." More tears filled his eyes and then spilled over. "It isn't that I haven't thought of you. Hopefully you know how much I have. This place is so... final."

He remained there in silence, just staring at the stone and gifts other people had left—people braver and kinder than him. Tears fell, and he continued doing nothing to stop them. He thought back over her life, remembering times from when she was a newborn all the way to high school. He didn't want to think about when she was sick. That wasn't her—that was the illness.

When the tears stopped, he placed his flowers against the stone. "I hope you like these," he said, "I think you would. They're beautiful. Just like you, both inside and outside." It took him a couple tries to get the flowers to stay up because his hands kept shaking.

He stood and then Jasmine took his hand, squeezing. Zachary wasn't sure how long he'd spent there, but she'd waited the entire time, not making a sound.

"Thank you," he said, his voice still unsteady. His eyes felt swollen, and he was sure they were red—in other words, he was a mess.

"Do you want more time?" she asked.

Zachary looked back over at the stone, now with their flowers against it, and shook his head. Part of him wanted to stay longer. Guilt punched him in the gut. How could he leave his baby sister there by herself? But at the same time, he knew she wasn't really there. If there was a Heaven, she was the life of the party. Maybe peeking down once in a while, keeping an eye on her troublesome brothers.

He walked away, looking at the stone until it was out of sight. He let out a long, deep breath and picked up his pace.

"It was healing, wasn't it?" Jasmine asked.

Zachary fought to find his voice, and his throat was raw. "Yes," was all he could manage.

They came up to a bench in the shade next to a water fountain. "Want to sit?" she asked.

His legs ached, so he sat without a word. Jasmine put her arm around him and he rested his face against his palms. All he could see was Sophia's face, and he wanted nothing more than to see her again and bring her home. Even though things were improving a lot for everyone—especially for his parents, who were now excited about their first grandchild and Brayden's engagement—it wasn't right without their sister. There would always be that empty place, and it would never again be filled or made right.

Finally, he turned to look at Jasmine. She had tears on her face, also.

"Are you okay?" he asked, his voice gruff.

She nodded. "I can't help but feel your pain."

His throat caught. "You're one of the few people who understands."

"Who wouldn't?" she asked. "I don't have to experience loss to see how much this hurts you."

Zachary leaned his head against her shoulder. He could think of one person who couldn't understand his heartache—Monica. But he didn't want to think about her anymore. She'd been a jerk, and their entire relationship had been all about her and her own issues. Sitting there with Jasmine, he finally believed it. It was time to move on and forget about all the horrible things she'd said to and about him.

He looked back at Jasmine, whose own eyes were red from watching Zachary in pain. She was the kind of girl he wanted to spend his time with—no, she was *the* girl.

"We should leave," he said, sitting up. "Dinner will be served soon, and everyone is sure to wonder where we are."

"If you're sure you're ready."

He nodded, ready as he was going to be. Whether or not he ever actually would be able to move on completely was yet to be seen, but he felt a step closer.

They walked back to the car, hand in hand. Neither spoke, but it felt comfortable. He was pretty sure Jasmine was thinking about her brother as much as he was thinking about Sophia. Maybe they could heal together.

She unlocked the passenger side. Zachary had forgotten that she had the keys still.

"You sit here. I'll drive again," she said.

"It sticks in second gear," he said, taking a seat.

"I noticed." She closed the door and went around to the driver's side. "This car has… character."

"It's embarrassing."

Jasmine started it. "No worse than anything I had growing up."

"Really?" He asked, surprised.

She nodded. "I didn't grow up in a house like yours, and I definitely didn't have a family like yours."

"Oh." What else could he say?

"It is what it is," she said as if reading his mind. "I'm making the best of it." She pulled out of the spot and they went back to his home in silence, with Sophia's music in the background. Zachary had turned it down, trying not to think about it being her playlist.

When they neared the road to his house, Zachary said, "I'm not quite ready to get back yet. There's a beach not too far away—it's pretty secluded this time of year. Would you mind going there first?"

"Point the way."

He gave her directions to a beach that only the locals went to. It tended to be empty during tourist season when most of the Kittle Falls residents were busy working, making the majority of their income in those busy months.

When they arrived, there was one car parked and Zachary could see a family down by the shore.

"I can't believe this place is so empty," Jasmine said as they walked toward the sand.

"It's Kittle Falls' best kept secret."

They walked toward the water in the opposite direction of the family. Zachary took his shoes off and walked in. Jasmine set her sandals by his shoes and joined him. They walked along quietly as the water splashed on their ankles. A bald eagle flew overhead.

"It's amazing out here," Jasmine whispered.

"This beach has always been a family favorite. I can't tell you how many times we've been out here—building sand castles as kids, throwing each other in the water, playing badminton or Frisbee." He sighed. "So many wonderful memories on this sand."

Jasmine smiled. "I'll bet."

Zachary laughed. "When Sophia was little, I would pick her up and run around making airplane noises. She would laugh and laugh, always begging for more. She was adored, and she knew it. Five older brothers who would do anything for her."

"It sounds like you guys gave her a wonderful life. So many people don't even find that in eighty years of life."

He nodded. That didn't make it fair, though.

Jasmine stood in front of him, taking both of his hands in hers. "Do you dance often?"

"Often?" Zachary asked. "Try never."

"What? How can that be? Not even a school dance?" She arched a brow.

"That wasn't really my scene, and besides, I have two left feet."

She splashed water away from his feet. "Nope. One right and one left. Let's try a simple dance."

Jasmine pressed herself against him. His heart raced with her so close. She let go of one hand and guided his hand to the small of her back and then she put her hand on his shoulder. "You're pretty tall, but I think this will work. Slow dances are a good way to start."

"Okay."

"Just follow my lead." She moved her feet, keeping their arms where they were. "You only have to focus on where your feet go, and we'll take it slowly."

They almost glided at the water's edge. Zachary managed to step on her feet several times. "I'm hopeless."

"Not at all. You just need practice."

"We'll see," he said. "Don't be surprised if I'm the first person you have to give up on."

Jasmine shook her head. "You have potential—you just need to tap into it, and that's where I come in. Here, move your foot out a bit... okay, perfect."

Before long, Zachary was surprised to find himself gliding along the shore with her like they were a couple of pros. Maybe not pros—at least not him, she obviously was as a dance instructor—but he was improving with each step, and finding that he enjoyed it. Or at least the company.

As they danced along his favorite beach, his heart warmed. Looking into Jasmine's eyes, he felt like he was right where he belonged.

Seventeen

⁓

"I HAD A WONDERFUL TIME with your family," Jasmine said, gazing into Zachary's eyes. After watching him mourn over his sister, it made her happy to see him laughing and joking with his family. She loved spending time with them. They were a large, happy group, and they accepted her with wide open arms, treating her as though she belonged, no questions asked.

Everything had been the opposite of her own family. Bright lights, a big, roomy house, lots of smiles and laughter. They teased each other, but each time it was in good-natured fun. Some of the brothers had some alcohol, but it was in moderation, and didn't affect the way anyone treated anyone else. Everyone continued laughing and being kind to one another. No yelling or brawls broke out.

Back home in the trailer, it didn't matter if they had a first time guest or not, after dinner, coarse joking and harsh words were always exchanged. No one ever walked away without a strong emotional and verbal beating.

The Hunter house—that was what Jasmine had always dreamed of growing up. She was sure that the family had their arguments, but it was nothing like she had grown up with. She could see the mutual respect ran deep among everyone.

Zachary took her hand and looked up at the stars. "It's a beautiful night and I'm with the most beautiful woman alive. I definitely had a wonderful time, too." He brushed his lips against hers, giving her the chills. He smelled of the ocean, reminding her of their dance session.

She wrapped her arms around him, kissing him back. Jasmine found herself wanting to stay in his arms forever.

He pulled back. "Where are you staying tonight?"

"At the shelter again, I suppose. I haven't heard anything about the building reopening." Not that she would have a place to stay, anyway, thanks to her mom.

"No, you're not."

"What do you mean?" she asked.

He shook his head. "I mean you're not staying there. We have spare rooms here, or if you don't feel comfortable staying where I am, I'm sure Jake and Tiffany would take you in. Or I could stay with Brayden. Either way, I'm not letting you go back there for another night."

"I don't know what to say, but I'll be fine."

Zachary shook his head, looking indignant. "I won't

allow it."

She smiled, liking the protective side of him. "Well, in that case, we'd better figure something out."

They went back inside and Zachary announced that Jasmine needed a place to stay.

Her face burned as everyone turned her way. She could feel their pity, and she hated nothing more.

Lana let go of Brayden's hand and came over to Jasmine. "What did you save from the fire?"

"Just the clothes on my back."

"You poor thing," Lana said, eyes wide. "How about we go shopping, and then you can stay with my family? I could use a sleepover, anyway."

Jasmine looked away, embarrassed. "I don't want to put you out."

"It'll be fun. What do you say? Shopping is always a good therapy."

Zachary nodded. "You should go."

Before she knew it, she and Lana were at a nearby mall, perusing through racks of clothes.

"I can't imagine losing everything," Lana said, holding up a sun dress. "Is the insurance going to pay to replace everything?"

"Hopefully. I have to call and find out what's going on. My roommate thinks we signed up for renter's insurance, but I can't remember." Jasmine froze, suddenly feeling bad that she had a house to sleep in and Kate was still at the shelter. Perhaps she could help her find someplace the next day.

"On the bright side," Lana said, bringing Jasmine back to the conversation, "you get a whole new wardrobe. How fun is that?" Lana smiled wide, her blonde hair falling into her face.

"I guess that's one way to look at it." Jasmine held up a shirt and seeing the price tag, shoved it back on the rack. She would need to order all new credit cards. She'd had a little cash in her pocket—that was how she'd gotten the flowers for Zachary to place on the grave— but there wasn't enough for even a pair of socks.

"That was fun," she said. "We'd better get back to your place."

"You haven't picked out any clothes," Lana said.

"I'll have to wait for my credit cards to be replaced." Jasmine shrugged. She might have to shower with her clothes on to wash them.

"Don't be silly," Lana said. "I'll get these."

Jasmine's eyes widened. "You'd do that?"

"Of course. What do you think of this dress? I think you'd look adorable—and Zachary wouldn't be able to take his eyes off you. Not that he didn't stop all night."

Her cheeks heated. "What? No he didn't. I look horrible. This is the outfit I put on yesterday."

"Didn't seem to bother him." Lana's bright eyes shone.

Looking away, Jasmine went over to the clearance rack and picked out a dress marked down to less than ten dollars.

"This one is cuter," Lana said about the regular-priced dress. "And I guarantee Zachary will be drooling."

"I don't know what I'll be able to afford after all of this is over."

"Then let me *give* it to you." Lana held it up to Jasmine. "Looks like it'll be a perfect fit. Want to try it on?"

Jasmine shrugged.

Lana handed it to her. "The dressing rooms are over there. I'll look for pajamas. You'll have to find your own intimates, though."

Jasmine tried to push away the humiliation of having someone she just met buying her clothes that she couldn't afford. Since she wouldn't have rent to pay, she could just pay Lana back after she got her next paycheck. She held her head up higher as she walked to the dressing rooms. She would just pay her back next week. Problem solved.

An hour later, she and Lana were headed for Lana's car, both of them loaded down with full shopping bags. Jasmine now had all the clothes and accessories she needed, including a toothbrush and hairbrush. It was amazing how much stuff was needed for just daily living.

When they got to her house, it was empty. "My parents must be out," Lana said. "I'll introduce you when they get back. You probably want to get into some clean clothes, don't you?"

"You have no idea."

Lana led her upstairs and then showed her an empty bedroom. "My sister was using this one, but she and her family left a few days ago, so make yourself at home. The bathroom is two doors down. Feel free to use all the hot water."

Jasmine thanked her and then dumped all the shopping bags onto the bed and started organizing them. She had enough clothes to get her through a week, and then she could wash everything and mix and match, creating new outfits. Lana had had a great time finding things that all went together and could be used together to make enough different outfits to last a month.

Jasmine wished she could get that excited over clothes. She had a fairly decent fashion sense, but had never had the money to enjoy many new clothes. All of her life, she had to deal with hand-me-downs and thrift store sales. Compared to her, everyone else had always been rich. She even felt rich just having a job where she was able to spend the money only on herself.

She wasn't sure how long she would stay with Lana's family—she didn't want to put them out—but she put the new clothes in the dresser drawers for the night, anyway. The long, hot shower relaxed her so much, she barely remembered to set the alarm for work the next day before she climbed into bed. If she was going to pay

Lana back, she couldn't afford to miss anymore work.

The hospital was taking care of her mom, and she'd said most of what she had to say. The rest didn't matter since her mom wouldn't listen, anyhow. If losing her son and causing fires that destroying the lives of strangers didn't get through to her, then nothing Jasmine said ever would, either. It never had before.

She fell into a deep, dreamless sleep. When her alarm went off, she felt rested, but still tired. It would probably take some time to readjust since she had gotten almost no sleep the night of the fire. After hitting snooze a couple times too many, she got up and dressed without taking a shower. She'd just had one the night before. How dirty could she be?

Her hair still smelled of Lana's shampoo and conditioner. She just needed to pull her hair back and put on a little makeup. Then she would be fine. It would be another day for heavy caffeine.

Jasmine sniffed. It smelled like someone had already started some. She went downstairs, finding an older gentleman sitting at the table in a plaid bathrobe, staring at a pile of large papers.

"Good morning," Jasmine said, hoping Lana's parents knew she was staying there.

He looked up and smiled, sticking a pencil behind his ear. "And a good morning to you, too. You must be Jasmine."

"I am." She went down the stairs and shook his

hand.

"Nice to meet you. I'm Dwight, Lana's dad. Sorry to hear about the fire."

"Thanks. It's like Lana said. I get to start over with a brand new wardrobe." Jasmine forced a smile.

"Sounds like my Lana. Both my girls would jump at the chance to buy all new clothes. We've got coffee if you want some and you can take anything you want from the fridge."

"Thank you." Jasmine went into the kitchen, found a mug, and poured some coffee. It was strong, and normally she would add milk and plenty of sugar. But this morning she appreciated the jolt of not only the caffeine, but the taste as well. It was the wakeup call she needed.

She drank it down and then grabbed a muffin from the fridge before calling out a goodbye to Dwight.

"Did Lana give you a key?"

Jasmine stopped. "No. I can just knock when I get back. It's okay."

"Nope," Dwight said, standing. "This is your home until you get something else squared away. Here's a key." He told her the code for the security system, too. "Come and go as you please, and if you need anything, just ask."

She started to feel choked up. Between the Hunters and Lana's family, Jasmine had never felt more cared about or taken care of before. "Thanks. I'll make myself useful. Clean toilets or something."

"Don't worry about it. You have enough on your plate. Have a good day."

"Bye." Jasmine looked at the time and hurried outside. She didn't have much time left to get to the gym after hitting snooze so many times.

When she got there, a new leotard, tights, and dance shoes sat where she usually put her purse. She looked around, confused. Whose were those? Had they hired someone to replace her?

Kate came in, giving her a hug. "Everyone came together and donated new dance stuff for us since we lost all of ours."

Jasmine hugged her back, feeling too emotional to say anything.

"Where'd you sleep last night?" Kate asked. "I never heard back from you."

Jasmine barely remembered receiving a text from Kate when she was eating dinner with the Hunters. "Sorry. I made a friend who insisted that I stay with her."

"Oh, good. I was worried, but figured you'd found something. Lisa from the Zumba department gave me a place to sleep. I might just stay there for the rest of the internship. Hopefully, that's okay with you. If you need someplace to stay, you could join me. It's a queen bed."

Jasmine gave Kate another hug. "I have a room to myself at Lana's house. I'm so glad you have one, too."

"We'll have to make an effort to stay in touch. I'm going to miss you if we never see each other."

"You owe me a double date, remember?" Jasmine asked.

"That's right, and you need to tell me more about that guy. What's his name again?"

"Zachary, and he—"

The door burst open and several little girls with tutus ran in. They shrieked, "Miss Jasmine!" and wrapped their little arms around her legs.

Kate laughed. "Guess I'll have to hear more about Zachary later. Better get back to my class, too."

Eighteen

ZACHARY TYPED AT HIS STORY with renewed vigor. He'd gotten up feeling like a new man that morning. Between facing his emotions—his true feelings, mainly fear—about Sophia's passing and having the support of Jasmine, he felt like he could do anything. He'd woken early without an alarm and had idea after idea for his story, and this time, the romantic theme came easily.

It was funny how a little real life inspiration could really make a difference. He wrote about Damion traveling through Europe, fighting for his life, but seeing the lady who'd joined him in a whole new light. Zachary's fingers flew, barely able to keep up with the ideas. It was invigorating, and Zachary hoped it lasted.

The sooner he could get to *The End*, the sooner his agent could start promoting the book and maybe, just maybe, someone from one of the publishing houses would take a look at it. It was a new day and a new book, so anything was possible.

Eventually, his stomach rumbled and his bladder

threatened to burst. He typed a few more words until he couldn't ignore his annoying basic needs. He backed up the document to his computer and the cloud before running to the bathroom and then to the kitchen.

The house was unusually quiet, meaning everyone had to be out for the day already. One look at the time told him he'd missed his chance to meet Jasmine for lunch. His heart sank, but maybe they could meet for dinner. Also, tomorrow was the weekend—wasn't it? He checked his phone's calendar. Today was Friday, so he and Jasmine could spend the entire day together tomorrow.

While he had his phone out, he sent her a quick text apologizing for not meeting her.

> *It's okay. Glad you're writing is going so well. I knew you'd get your groove back.*
> *I really have. It's amazing. There's nothing like it.*

Jasmine sent a string of dancing and cheering smilies. *I can't wait to read it.*

> *It's going to be a while before it's even close to ready.*

No problem. I still have to finish the first one. A couple hearts followed.

He sent some hearts, also. *How's your day going? I really wanted to see you.*

> *Me, too. It's good. It was so relaxing to actually sleep in a bed, and then some coworkers got me new*

dance clothes.

Wow, that's awesome. I'm so glad things are turning around for you. No one deserves it more.

Oh, you're too sweet. Dancing hearts followed.

I mean it. I'm not keeping you from anything, am I?

Not yet. My class is going to start soon, though. I'm just sitting on your bench watching some birds.

My bench? Zachary laughed. *I didn't realize I had a bench.*

It's the one you always sit at near my classroom.

Ah, I see.

Wish I could keep chatting. Gotta get to my class.

Glad we could talk. Kind of. He sent some laughing smilies.

Me, too. Can't wait to see you again. I miss you.

His heart skipped a beat. *I miss you, too.*

Oh, and keep writing! Don't lose your flow.

Zachary's heart warmed. Having her support meant everything. It was hard to believe a week ago, he didn't even know her. The days since meeting her had changed him, and now he would do anything for her, and to keep her.

She already believed in him and wanted to be there

for him, but he wanted to do more for her, too. He hadn't really even done anything to deserve all of her support and kindness. Especially with her being down on her luck with the fire, this was his chance to give back. But how? What could he do?

He stuck some leftovers in the microwave and looked out the window, trying to figure it out. He didn't have much money, and what little he did have was quickly dwindling away—it was worth it. He had spent it all on Jasmine.

After eating, he went back to his laptop and wrote a bunch of notes for what he wanted to write for the rest of the novel, and then turned off the computer. It was getting late, but he needed to head over to the Hunter Family Store and see if they needed any help. Even if he could earn just twenty bucks, he could take Jasmine out somewhere that night.

Zachary looked in the mirror. He didn't look great, but well enough to head for the store. He didn't want to waste any time in the shower. It was time for action.

He jumped in his car and sped off for the shop. He had to park a block away, but it was better than walking from home. There was no time to waste. When he got inside, Cruz was stocking shelves and Jake was with some kid at the registers taking care of a long line of customers.

Zachary went over to Cruz. "Need any help?"

"Hey, bro." He held out his fist and Zachary

bumped it with his. "Strapped for cash?"

"You know it," Zachary said. "I want to take Jasmine out tonight, but I can't even afford ice cream."

"Fill out a punch card in the back room and then grab a box. We have a ton of inventory to stock, so your timing couldn't be better, yo."

"Good." Zachary went to the back room, not surprised to see that it looked exactly the same as it had in high school. Some things never changed, and that was actually kind of comforting. He found a punch card, stuck it in the time clock, and jumped when clicked loudly, stamping the card. Something else that didn't change.

He filled out his name and address, and then stuck it in a slot on the wall. He turned around and saw the pile of boxes. Had all the vendors delivered that day? Glancing over the labels, he found one with items near where Cruz was stocking shelves. That way, they could talk while filling the shelves. It would be good to catch up, and it would make the time go by faster.

Zachary picked up the box and headed back to where Cruz sat.

"Oh, good. You've got another box, and I was worried we'd run out," Cruz joked.

"Yeah, right," Zachary said. "We could work until closing and still have boxes left over." He pulled out his pocketknife and broke the seal of the box. He pulled out some snack items and stuck them on the shelf.

"Jasmine seems nice," Cruz said. "Is it serious?"

Zachary paused. "Seems to be going in that direction. I've never met anyone like her."

"I'm starting to feel left out." Cruz stood, flattening his box. He shoved it behind Zachary's box and then took some snacks out of it and put them on the shelf.

"You looking for a girlfriend?" Zachary asked.

"Not a chance, dude. All the rest of you could have cute little families, and I'd still be happy living the single life. You know my plan, right?"

"Open a tattoo shop?" Zachary asked.

"Yeah. Ideally, I'd like to find a place that could double as a home and a parlor. Like, I could live in the back or the second level. With the late hours, it'd be nice to already be home."

Zachary put more snacks on the shelf and realized the box was already empty. "Where are you looking?"

"Lemme grab another box first." Cruz flattened the box and took both back into the back room, coming out with a new one. He pulled out his knife and opened it. "I was looking at some places not too far away, but ran into issues with zoning."

"You've made it that far?" Zachary asked, impressed.

"Dude, yeah. I want this as bad as Brayden wants his urgent care clinic. It's just that Kittle Falls is less excited about a tat parlor than health care."

"I can see that. They're probably worried about the type of people it'll attract."

"But what I'm trying to get them to see is it'll bring in serious revenue. They have no idea." Cruz shoved a box of candies on the shelf harder than necessary.

"Can you have the business be something else that just happens to also provide tattoos?" Zachary asked.

"If I have to, but I want to be true to my dream, man."

Zachary grabbed another bunch of snacks from the box. "Even Brayden had to do things differently than he wanted. Change some things up."

"Yeah, I know. I just have things in my mind the way I want them, and that's how I want them."

Knowing Cruz, that wasn't surprising. "Hey, I understand. Really, I do. Look at my book. I wouldn't put romance in when that's what the publishers demanded, and now look at me. Back home with Mom and Dad, sleeping in the same bed I did in the first grade."

Cruz shrugged. "And now they're stoked. All of us are back in town. It's not all bad."

"Neither is a little compromise." Zachary folded the empty box and then the two of them went into the back room and got some more boxes.

"Then write a romance." Cruz arched an eyebrow, the corners of his mouth twitching.

Zachary laughed. "I'm not writing a romance. I did write *some* romance into my second novel—look at that. I did compromise."

Cruz shook his head. "Now that I have to read."

"You should. You'd probably like it." Zachary thought of how much their mom had been bugging Cruz to find a girlfriend. "Maybe it'll even inspire you to get a girlfriend," he teased.

Cruz gave him a little shove. "You've been listening to Mom too long."

"Just sayin'."

"Hey, Jake," Cruz called, glancing toward the registers. "You need Zachary, here, to help you with the customers?"

Jake turned their way. "Actually, yeah. Calvin has to leave early and Bella can't come until her regular time."

Cruz eyed Zachary. "Go bug Jake."

"Whatever. You'll find your dream coming true faster if you're willing to give a little. Just think about it."

"If I'm looking for advice, I'll let you know." Cruz turned back to the shelf, cramming candies on.

Zachary felt bad. He hadn't meant to upset Cruz. His brother was usually so good natured, always laughing and teasing. It was a little unsettling to have upset him.

"What's with Cruz?" Jake asked as Zachary came around to the other side of the counter.

"Don't talk to him about his tattoo shop."

"I could have told you that," Jake said. "It's a sensitive subject at the moment. The city council is giving him a lot of grief over the whole thing. They want him to take it somewhere else, but you know Cruz."

"His way or the highway."

"That's our Cruz."

The rest of the afternoon flew by as the shop stayed busy with tourists coming and going. It was nice to catch up with Jake during the small breaks they had. With Jake married and living in his own house, Zachary hadn't seen as much of him since coming back to town.

"How's Tiffany?" he asked.

"She's good, but she's been getting sick a lot, so not able to help out here as much. I'm really glad you came by."

"Always good to be broke." Zachary laughed.

"If you need extra cash, we definitely need the help here. I don't want to put any pressure on Tiffany. She doesn't have morning sickness. It's more like all-day sickness."

"That sucks. She seemed okay at dinner last night."

"Did you notice she barely ate anything?" Jake asked.

"No, sorry."

Another rush of customers came, and before he knew it, it started to get dark outside. He'd missed another meal with Jasmine. He pulled out his phone—of course, a missed text. Sighing, he checked it.

Lana's family invited me to out to dinner with them. Can we get together tomorrow?

Zachary sat down. "What a relief," he mumbled.

Jake turned to him, giving him a curious look.

"Jasmine."

"How's that going?" Jake asked. "She seems to like you a lot."

"I'd like to keep it that way."

"When Tiffany feels better, we'll have you guys over. That'll be a date you don't have to pay for."

Zachary rose and leaned against the counter. "How did you convince Tiffany to stay in town?"

"How could she resist this?" Jake waved his hands up and down in front of himself.

Zachary burst out laughing. "I've missed your humor."

"You think I was joking?" Jake looked hurt.

"Stop."

Jake grinned. "Seriously, I don't know. She didn't want to stay, that's for sure. Not at first, anyway."

"I need to figure something out," Zachary said. "Her internship ends at the end of the summer, and that's not far away."

"Win her over, Zachary. Make it so that nothing else looks as good compared to being with you. Use your smile—every one of us has been jealous of that since birth."

"You have?" Zachary wasn't convinced, though he'd heard it all his life.

"Sometimes you can be so dense." Jake gave him a playful punch. "Girls have always fallen over themselves when you smile. At the risk of sounding flowery, you've got a smile that lights up a room."

Zachary shoved him. "You do sound flowery, and I'm the writer."

"Use it to your advantage. We all have something. You're creative and have that grin. Put them together and make Jasmine want to stay in Kittle Falls. I saw the way she looks at you. It won't take much."

Nineteen

~

Jasmine's smart phone beeped, letting her know the battery was about to die. She groaned. It was horrible timing. She was getting close to the end of Zachary's story, and she didn't want to put it down.

She turned off the screen and went to find her plug. The one that had been in her scorched condo. The fire was proving to be more and more of a headache each time she realized she needed something that was now ashes. What were the chances that someone in the house had a matching plug?

Jasmine went downstairs and found Dwight and Susan watching a movie. Lana was out helping Brayden with something for his clinic.

"I hate to bother you," Jasmine said, "but I need to plug my phone in and I don't have a charger anymore."

"Let's see what we can do," Susan said. She aimed the remote at the TV, pausing the movie. "Mine's down here already, so let's give that a try first." She went over to the kitchen and Jasmine followed.

Susan held up the end of the cord. "Does this look like the right shape?"

Jasmine looked at it, unsure. "Can I try it?"

"Sure." Susan handed it to her.

Jasmine tried fitting it, but it was too big.

"Dwight, where's yours?" Susan called.

"In the dining room."

"Of course." Susan went over to the dining room table and found the charger under a pile of his papers. "Try this one, dear."

Jasmine slid it into her phone. It was a perfect fit. "Can I use it upstairs?"

"Go right ahead." She handed it to Jasmine. "Did you call about the insurance? All of this stuff should be replaced. And soon, I would think."

"No. I got busy. I'd call tomorrow, but they'll be closed on the weekend. Maybe I'll leave a message and try back on Monday."

"Just get it taken care of, sweetie. They surely have a time limit, and you've already been through enough."

Jasmine gave her a weak smile. "Thanks. I will."

Susan put her hand on Jasmine's arm. "Don't think I'm rushing you out. You're welcome here as long as you need a place. I just don't want to see you taken advantage of. Insurance companies will take money all day long, but they hate paying it out."

"I appreciate it." And she really did. It was nice to receive some motherly advice—she'd never gotten any growing up, unless the occasional concerned teacher counted.

"If you need anything, just let us know. We'd be happy to help." Susan smiled and then went back to her movie with Dwight.

Jasmine watched them snuggled on the couch together. She tried to imagine what her life would have been like had her parents been like that. Not just sitting together, but seeming to enjoy each other's company after probably more than thirty years together. No cigarettes, yelling, or cursing. Nothing broken to step around.

Jasmine shook her head and hurried up to her room. She plugged in the phone as close to the bed as she could. She opened the reading app and picked up where she'd left off. Because of the cord, she had to lay at a funny angle, but the only thing she cared about was getting to the end and finding out what happened to Damion. If she ended up sore or with a kinked neck, it would be worth it.

Her pulse raced as she read the final chapters. After she finished, she rolled over onto her back, trying to breathe normally again. Zachary was a seriously talented writer. They just needed to get the book into people's hands. The publishers might not give it a chance, but readers would love it—and clamor for the next one. She was already itching to read it, even though it wasn't fully written yet.

There was a knock on the door. Did Dwight need his charger already? She sat up, looking at her phone. It was only at fifty percent. That was better than nothing.

She opened the door, but Lana stood there instead. "How are you?" she asked, smiling.

"Worn out." Jasmine ran a hand through her hair.

Lana raised an eyebrow. "From what? Mind if I come in?"

Jasmine stepped back, allowing her into the room, and then closed the door. "How's Brayden?"

"Getting a little stressed. Everything is coming together for the clinic, but he's getting tripped up over some of the details. I told him there are a lot of things that need to come together and he's better off relaxing, but those Hunter boys." She shook her head, blonde waves getting in her eyes.

"What?" Jasmine asked.

"They're perfectionists. Haven't you noticed?"

Jasmine thought about it. "Yeah, I guess I can see that."

"I'm not saying it's a bad thing," Lana said. "It can just be a little annoying at times. I'm a big picture kind of girl, so I don't get it, but I do appreciate his attention to detail. Someone has to." She shrugged. "I guess that's where balancing each other out comes into play."

"Sounds like you two are perfect for each other."

Lana beamed. Then she turned her attention back to Jasmine. "So, why are you so worn out? You never said."

"I just finished Zachary's book. I feel like I've been through a war." Jasmine giggled.

"Is that a good thing?"

"Yeah. The book is so good. I could see everything like I was watching a movie, only it was more intense."

"And that's the one the publishers won't even look at?" Lana asked.

Jasmine nodded. "They don't know what they're missing."

"You guys have to show them."

"What do you mean?" Jasmine asked. "How can we do that? His agent couldn't even do that, and it's her job."

"I've got a cousin who's an author, and she's been selling her books online herself. She writes things that she says publishers would never touch, but people love it. She sells hundreds of copies every month of each one and has cut back her hours at work. Actually, I keep waiting to hear she's quit."

"Really?" Jasmine asked. "What does she write?"

Lana looked away, seeming embarrassed. "I probably should read some of it, huh? She's my cousin. Well, she describes it as *Little House on the Prairie* meets *Star Trek* meets zombies."

"Come again?" Jasmine asked.

Lana laughed. "I know it sounds weird, but there's an audience."

"If that's the case, then Zachary would make a killing. His thriller has mass appeal."

"You think he'd be open to trying online sales?" Lana asked. "I mean, if Erin can find an audience, it sounds like he really could."

"I have no idea. He seems pretty intent on getting a deal."

"That might be his in for publishing, though. Erin said publishers sometimes go after authors who are doing really well selling ebooks."

Jasmine scratched her head. "I wonder if Zachary knows that."

"You should find out. I don't know any more than I just told you, but it might be the answer he's looking for."

"Would you be willing to talk to your cousin?" Jasmine asked. "I'll see if Zachary's interested."

"Yeah, sure. If his book is as good as you say, he'll probably do fantastic."

Jasmine's eyes lit up. "Thanks for telling me about that."

"No problem. I'll call her tomorrow and let you know what she says."

"Perfect." Excitement rose from Jasmine's core. That was the answer—she just knew it. That was exactly how to get people reading—and talking about—his book. Word would spread like wildfire. Then he either wouldn't need a big publisher or they would come crawling to him. Begging. She grinned, just thinking about the look on his face when everyone loved his book as much as she did. He would be absolutely thrilled.

Lana smiled. "Goodnight." She left the room.

A new text came in. It was from Zachary.

We still on for tomorrow?

I wouldn't miss it. I have exciting news, too.

Really? What?

She wanted to tell him, but not over a text. *I'll tell you tomorrow.*

Sounds good. What time works for you?

They discussed the details and when she thought the conversation was over, she got a new text.

I really missed you today.

Her heart swelled in her chest and heat rose into her face.

I couldn't stop thinking about you, either.

Tomorrow's going to be the best. Leave the whole day open.

Jasmine's heart raced. *I will. Goodnight.*

Goodnight. Hugging smilies followed the message.

She smiled wide. He was the sweetest thing. How had she gotten so lucky?

Jasmine got up and got ready for bed. When she sat down, she noticed a missed text.

Is it tomorrow yet? I miss you already. I just want to see your beautiful face.

She held the phone close to her heart. He was perfect… and now she'd probably be up all night thinking about him.

I wish it was tomorrow already. Miss you, too. A whole bunch. Can't wait to see your smiling face.

He sent her a bunch of dancing hearts.

Jasmine's heart fluttered. She found a bunch of cutesy animations and sent them to him.

She leaned back against the pillow, happier than she'd ever been. She had never experienced anything like this. Pure, unadulterated happiness. Meeting Zachary had changed everything—everything!

All day, she'd been walking with a bounce in her step despite dealing with the fallout from the fire and knowing that her mom was in the hospital only a half an hour away. Nothing else mattered except that the most wonderful guy alive liked her. Her!

She picked up her phone and read through the texts again, her heart warming her wholly. This was the life she wanted. She didn't care if she had to work at the gym in Kittle Falls her whole life. She adored the girls who came and went, and spending time with Zachary was far better than working at one of those prestigious dance studios in Portland. If they wouldn't take her for an internship, who was to say they'd even consider her for an actual position?

Jasmine's eyes grew heavy as her heart continued to feel lighter. She could live like this forever.

Her phone rang, and she sat up, eager to hear Zachary's voice. As wonderful as his texts were, they didn't compare to hearing his voice.

She accepted the call without looking. "Hello?" she asked with a song to her voice.

"Is this Jasmine Blackwell?"

Her heart sank. "Yes. Who is this?"

"My name is Kathy McNight. I'm the head nurse on your mother's floor."

There was nothing like the reminder of her mom to sour her perfect mood. "Okay."

"You're her daughter, correct?"

Unfortunately. "Yes. Can I help you?"

"She's having a bit of a breakdown and we want to calm her down without sedating her if possible. Can you tell us anything that would help her relax?"

"Have you tried nicotine or alcohol?" Jasmine asked, not bothering to keep the sarcasm out of her voice.

"What? No. Is she addicted to either?"

Didn't the nurses communicate? She'd told the other one she wanted her mom to get into a rehab center. Jasmine took a deep breath before responding. "Try both, and probably more. I wouldn't know for sure. Have you called my dad?"

"We don't have that information. She doesn't want him involved."

Jasmine sighed. "Just sedate her. That's your best option. I can't imagine what she's like without any of her vices."

"Would you be able to come to the hospital and see her? That might help."

She glanced at the time. "No, I really can't. It wouldn't help, anyway. We've been estranged for years until she showed up at my door and burned down an entire building."

"Oh. I see." Click-clacking of a computer keyboard sounded through the phone. "I see a note here in her file that the police have questioned her and have grounds for arrest."

Jasmine's eyes widened. Maybe *that* was the wakeup call her mom needed to straighten out. "That's not surprising."

"But I see here they're willing to drop the charges if she successfully completes a rehabilitation program."

"What does she think about that?" Jasmine asked.

"Hold on a sec, dear."

Elevator music played in Jasmine's ear. She took several deep breaths to try and calm herself. The music finally stopped.

"Jasmine?" asked Kathy.

"Yes."

"I spoke with your mother's nurse for the night, and

apparently the officers' visit is what started her fit in the first place. She doesn't want to go to jail or rehab. But she has no choice."

"Can't you guys explain that she can have freedom once she finishes rehab?" Jasmine asked, fatigue coursing through her body.

"Several members of our staff have tried, and she just gets more upset."

"Trust me, she won't listen to me, either."

"You sure you can't come down here?" asked the nurse. "It would really help her out to see a familiar face."

Jasmine had seen her mom throw fits before, and it always resulted in someone hurt or something broken. Always. And that was when she had access to her precious cigarettes and beer. Without them? That wasn't a sight Jasmine wanted to witness.

"Sorry. I need to get sleep for work tomorrow. I can't miss another day on her account." She groaned. The call had her so flustered she'd accidentally lied. She didn't have any classes the next day.

The nursed sighed into the phone. "All right. I understand. But you do understand that will result in your mother being sedated?"

"Yes. It's sad to say, but I'm sure that would be in everyone's best interest, including her own. She might even feel better after a good sleep."

"Sedation isn't exactly like falling asleep naturally,

Miss Blackwell."

The nurse could be as mean as she wanted, but she simply didn't understand. "It's your call. Without her vices, her fit isn't going to improve. Maybe she'll even manage to change her mind about rehab after that."

"Well, thank you for at least considering coming down. Goodnight."

"You too," Jasmine said and ended the call. So much for her good mood—leave it to her parents to find a way to ruin any good she managed to find in her life. Even moving away and paying to keep her information private hadn't helped.

She gritted her teeth. This time, they wouldn't win. She would have a good night and not let her mom's dramatics get the best of her. She wasn't sure if Zachary was her boyfriend or not, but what they had was better than anything she'd ever had in her whole life. Maybe tomorrow she would find out if they were officially a couple.

Twenty

~

ZACHARY SQUEEZED GEL ONTO HIS hand and rubbed it between his palms before running it through his hair. He looked pretty good if he did say so himself. He couldn't wait to pick up Jasmine, and he broke into a smile just thinking about seeing her. It had been torturous staying away the day before, even though time had passed fairly quickly in the shop with his brothers.

But now he at least had some money to spend on her, giving her the best date she'd ever seen. His parents had not only paid him for the day's work, but also an advance for the next week. Zachary had gotten himself a haircut, a new shirt, and new shoes. He felt like a new man, and he still had plenty of money left over to shower Jasmine with gifts all day long.

He stared at himself in the mirror again, and his smile remained. He tried to look at himself from an outsider's perspective. He could see what Jake said about his smile. He figured it had been one of those things family said to make him feel better when he was down.

But maybe there was something to it after all.

He smiled wider, but it looked goofy—fake. He thought about Jasmine again, and his smile really did brighten his face. He felt like a dork smiling in the mirror, but it was good practice. Not that he needed to pretend to be happy to see her.

He would probably leap into the air with joy. It didn't matter what anyone else thought. He adored Jasmine and she seemed to return the feelings. That alone was worth celebrating.

Zachary found some mouthwash under the sink and swished as long as he could stand the burn. He remembered when he and his brothers were teenagers, they would put as much in their mouths as they could just to see who could swish it around the longest. It had been a test of manhood.

He started to laugh, remembering, realizing only then how funny of a test it was. Blue liquid dripped out of his mouth and he spit it out into the sink before it ended up all over the mirror. It wouldn't have been the first time.

The boys often tried to get each other to laugh and spit out the mouthwash first, and with Cruz always making people laugh, mouthwash had ended up decorating not only the mirror, but the walls at times, too. Many times. He remembered one time Cruz, at about nine years old, was dancing around like a monkey, determined to make Brayden laugh. All of the boys had about died laughing. Mouthwash ended up all over the bathroom. Not one of them had made it into the sink.

Even though it had been years earlier, and Zachary had matured, he burst out laughing as if back in the moment. He sat on the closed toilet, trying to keep from laughing too loudly.

Zachary managed to calm himself, grateful for the good memories. Ever since Sophia's passing, it seemed like the happy times with his family had been too easily forgotten.

He looked back in the mirror to make sure he looked okay. He wiped some tears away from his eyes, shaking his head at himself. Laughing about a fifteen year old mess—had he grown up at all?

Running his hands through his hair one more time, he tried to forget about the old incident, but the more he tried to forget, the more alive the memory became. He laughed again, his stomach aching.

It was a good thing he was going to spend the day with Jasmine. She would get his mind off the Hunter boys' old test of manhood.

Zachary walked out of the bathroom, his mind fully focused on Jasmine's beautiful face. When he reached the kitchen and saw Cruz, he lost it again, and burst into laughter uncontrollably remembering Cruz dancing like a monkey.

His mom turned him, stirring something on the stove. "What's so funny?"

Zachary glanced back over at Cruz, making eye contact. He doubled over in laughter, clutching his stomach. Gaining control, he stood up and looked around. He cleared his throat.

Cruz arched a pierced brow. "Am I missing something?"

"Don't ask." Zachary grabbed a plate from the cupboard and sat across from his brother.

"Whatever, dude." Cruz drank his orange juice.

Rafael came into the kitchen. "What's so funny? It sounded like a pack of hyenas in here."

"Ask him," Cruz said, nodding toward Zachary.

Zachary took some toast from a plate in the middle of the table and buttered it. "I was in the bathroom and remembered that time we were doing one of those mouthwash contests and Cruz was dancing like a monkey. We all laughed so hard we spread it all over the walls."

Rafael laughed. "I'd forgotten all about those contests. Mom was so mad that day. Remember?"

"Was that time you boys spit mouthwash all over the bathroom?" she asked, not looking amused.

Cruz joined in the laughter. "I smelled like mint for a week. And someone got it in my ear."

"I had it up my nose," Rafael said. "You think that stuff burns in your mouth? Let me tell you, you haven't experienced anything until it's in your nasal cavity."

Zachary's eyes watered from laughter. "Water's bad

enough."

"You were the one laughing at me over it." Rafael shook his head.

"Never a dull moment with you boys," their mom said. "Should I make more eggs?"

Cruz filled his plate with what was left on the table. "Yeah, if these guys want to eat. I gotta get to the shop."

"Thanks," Zachary said, shaking his head at Cruz. "We can always count on you."

"You know it." Cruz scarfed down the eggs and got up. "See you guys. You going to the shop today, Zachary?"

He shook his head. "Not today. I have a date."

"Jasmine?" Rafael asked.

"Who else?" Zachary asked. He took some more toast and ate quickly, eager to pick her up. When he was done, he rose.

"Where do you think you're going?" asked his mom.

"To pick up Jasmine. Why?"

"You said you wanted eggs."

"Right." Zachary sat, feeling like he was five again. Funny how family could do that.

He waited for the eggs and ate enough to keep his mom happy, even though he wasn't hungry anymore. His mom turned around over the stove. Rafael nodded toward the door, indicating for Zachary to make his escape.

Zachary whispered a quick thanks and ran out the

door. He stopped cold when he got outside. Jasmine sat across the yard in the swinging bench they had sat on the other day. What was she doing there? Zachary was supposed to pick her up.

She didn't see him, as she appeared to be reading something on her phone. He walked over, careful to be quiet and not step on twigs. When he reached her, he stood, watching her. She was so beautiful, and she appeared to be enjoying what she read—and she was into it enough that she hadn't noticed him.

He cleared his throat.

Jasmine jumped and then looked up. "I didn't hear you."

Zachary smiled. "I didn't know you were coming over."

"I wanted to surprise you, but it looks like you got me."

"Oh, I'd say you definitely surprised me." He smiled again.

She put her phone on the bench, bounced up, and wrapped her arms around him. She smelled sweet, kind of like citrus. He wrapped his arms around her, putting his face against her hair, and breathed in deeply, holding her tight.

"I missed you," he whispered.

She looked at him. "Your texts were so sweet. I couldn't wait to see you. I hope it's okay that I came over. I just didn't want to wait another minute."

"I can't complain about that."

Jasmine kissed his cheek. "So, what's the plan for today? You didn't really tell me anything."

His heart raced. "I've got quite a bit planned. I hope you've left your calendar wide open."

"That I did, and I'm excited to see what you have in store. Although, I'd be happy just sitting here on this seat with you all day."

"Really?" he asked.

"Yeah, you could tell me stories."

"Have you been reading my novel again?" he asked.

Her eyes lit up. "Reading? I finished it already, and it was amazing. I can't believe you wrote it—seriously, it's better than most books I've read. Better than a lot of movies, too."

Zachary stared at her, trying to comprehend what he'd heard. "You don't have to say that."

"I'm not just saying it. If I thought it needed improvement, I'd tell you where. I promise."

"That means so much to me." He ran his fingers along her jaw, staring into her eyes.

She stared into his eyes. "You should publish it."

He laughed. "Why didn't I think of that?"

"No. I mean *you* should publish it. Sell it as an ebook and get attention on it. Then—"

He froze, dropping his fingers from her face. "No. I want a publishing deal with a company, Jasmine. I've had my sights set on it since I was little, and I know that it can take some time to get something accepted. I'm fine with it. That's just the way it goes. I may have to write a couple first, but the good thing about that is that I'll have a backlist to draw from. I won't have to go crazy writing things later."

"But you can—"

Zachary put his lips on hers and then pulled back. "I love that you're this excited about my book, but I'm really okay with the process. The fact that I met you after I had to come back here only proves that I'm on the right path. It's all going to work out, even if it takes time. I'll keep working at it as long as I need to."

"I just want to see you succeed. You'll make a killing. I know you will." Her eyes lit up.

He kissed her again, his heart fluttering. "Your support means more than you could ever know. Even just spending time with you helps. I'm making a lot of progress on this second novel. I've never written so fast in my life—you're a true inspiration."

"Really?" she whispered.

"Of course, but I didn't ask you on a date to stand in my parents' yard talking about my writing. Are you ready to start the day?"

"Like I said, as long as I'm with you, I'm happy."

Zachary slid his fingers down to her chin, lifted it, kissing her again. "I could do this all day."

Her cheeks turned pink. "So could I."

He kissed her again, and then he heard whistling

from behind. Zachary turned around to see Rafael waving.

"Having fun, you two?" Rafael teased.

"Yes, we are," Jasmine called, smiling. She gave Zachary a quick kiss. "Thanks for asking, Rafael."

Zachary snickered. She fit in perfectly with his family.

Twenty-One

BUTTERFLIES FLURRIED AROUND IN JASMINE'S stomach as Zachary ordered his dinner from across the table. It had been the perfect day, starting out at the beach with some fancy ice cream cones coated in chocolate, caramel, and marshmallow.

When they were done, Zachary had taken her hand and ran with her along the edge of the water, splashing ocean water on their legs. Then he surprised her by picking her up. She shrieked and held on for dear life, fearful—but also kind of hoping—he would fall and they would tumble down together.

He hadn't, though. Zachary had kept his balance while running with her in his arms. Then he'd set her down, and they had wandered the beach, hand in hand, stopping at all the little shows. A dog jumped through hula hoops. A baby monkey rode backwards on a pig. Some little girls juggled half a dozen bowling pins each.

Just as she grew hungry, he received a text, blindfolded her, and took her to a little field where a beautiful picnic sat waiting for them. Later, he'd told her that he'd talked Jake and Rafael into setting it up. She and Zachary had eaten a delicious meal prepared by one of his favorite local restaurants.

Then they'd gone to a movie, had whatever snacks she wanted—which hadn't been much after such a delicious meal. She'd overeaten because it had all been so good. After the movie was over, they toured a store that made candy and got free samples of taffy, which had been ridiculously sweet and tasty.

After that, when she thought the day couldn't be any better, he'd taken her to a store outside of town filled with gorgeous dresses and told her to pick any one of her choosing. Zachary said he wanted to help her replace her wardrobe and to make sure she had something she adored. He'd stepped outside, whispering something to the manager. She'd spent nearly an hour trying on dresses, with the lady helping her assuring her that she had plenty of time.

Now, they sat in a beautiful restaurant, next to a flowing fountain, not too far away from some live music. Soft, sweet melodies had been playing since they arrived. Jasmine glanced down at her beautiful new dress, feeling the soft fabric as she crossed one leg over the other.

Zachary turned to her. "What would you like to eat?"

Jasmine turned to the waiter and gave him her order, and then he hurried off. She turned back to Zachary. "This whole day has been beyond anything I had hoped for. I can't believe the lengths you went to in preparing this."

He smiled, melting her on the spot. "You deserve nothing less than the best, and with everything going on lately, it's been challenging to spend time with you, much less attempting to give you what you deserve."

"I don't feel like I deserve any of this," she admitted.

Zachary reached across the table and took her hand. "Yes you do, and so much more." He rubbed his thumb over her knuckles, giving her the chills. "I wish I could give you everything you wanted, but I hope this comes close."

She put her other hand on top of his. "It's more, far more. You've made me feel like a princess."

He lifted her hand and kissed it, first on the back of it, then on each knuckle. "I'm so lucky to have met you, Jasmine. I hope this day has helped make your stay in Kittle Falls a little brighter." It seemed like he wanted to say more, but he just stared into her eyes.

"You have," she whispered. "I'll never forget today, even if I get old and forget everything else."

His heart-melting smile widened. "And that goes double for me."

The appetizers arrived, and he let go of her hands. "I hope you're hungry."

She was, and she also hoped she would have time to

exercise the next day. Instead, she smiled back and said, "Of course. Everything looks delicious." He had ordered enough appetizers to feed his entire family.

They ate food so fancy Jasmine had never heard of, much less seen or tasted. She tried a little bit from each plate, her mouth watering for more. She would lose her dancer's figure if she kept this up, but she couldn't bring herself to stop. It was the ideal end to their flawless dream date.

Zachary told funny stories from his life growing up in Kittle Falls with five siblings, and Jasmine loved all of it. He was a delightful storyteller in person—not that it was any big surprise. Then he turned it around and asked questions about her. Unfortunately, talking about her childhood was the last thing she wanted to do, especially on this most wonderful of days.

He didn't seem put off by her short answers, and instead asked her about her dancing career. A topic she was far more eager to talk about. He seemed genuinely interested in hearing about how she'd traveled around the country participating in various performances.

The food arrived and Jasmine realized she'd already stuffed herself. The meal smelled and looked delicious, and even made her mouth water when the steam and smells came to her face, but her stomach twisted in knots, begging her not to eat anymore.

Zachary dug in, and like many guys she'd met, he seemed to have a bottomless pit for a stomach. She picked at her food, moving it around the plate more than she actually ate.

When the meal was over, he asked her if she wanted to walk along the beach. "There's a small one not far from here that most people know nothing about. I don't know about you, but I could stand to walk some of this food off."

"I'd love to."

The waiter came by and Zachary asked him to box up what was left and keep it chilled while they went to the beach.

"Of course, sir." The waiter walked away.

"They'll keep it chilled for you?" Jasmine asked, surprised. "I've never heard of that."

"People love to go for walks after eating here. Usually, they go to a different beach than I'm going to take you, but in order to keep the food fresh, they have a special refrigeration unit just for customer's leftovers."

"That's crazy, but also really cool."

"It's one of the things that draws people here. Who wants to box up their food on a hot evening and then stick in their car? This solves that problem, and I think it makes this place all the more attractive."

"No more than you." She smiled.

"Or you." He took her hand.

When they left, just before going out the door, one of the staff stopped them and took their picture in front of a beautiful potted tree.

"We'll have that ready for you when you return for your food."

"Thank you," Zachary said and then took Jasmine's hand again.

"Is that another one of their many services?" she asked.

"No. I asked them specifically to take our picture and print it out for us. They were most accommodating."

Jasmine squeezed his hand. "And you're most thoughtful. I can't believe any of this—really."

"Is it too much?" he asked.

"Not at all. I feel like royalty. I'm just not used to it."

"You should. I want you to feel like the most special woman alive."

Heat crept into her face, and then she nodded. "You have." She truly felt unworthy.

They went back into his car and drove for about ten minutes before pulling off the road. "Like I said, not many people know about this particular beach."

He wrapped his arm around her and then they stepped over logs and branches. Jasmine was careful not to damage her new dress as they made their way to the private, little beach.

After they stepped over the last log, she let out a breath. "It's gorgeous."

"Isn't it? Sorry about the logs, though. It wasn't always this challenging to get here. I think some storms must have made it worse."

She stared at the water. "Don't apologize. It was good exercise."

"Speaking of," he rubbed her palm with his thumb and then led her toward the water. They walked along the edge of the water, close enough to feel the spray of water, but not actually walking in it.

"I've had the most wonderful day," Jasmine said.

"Me, too. I want to give you more days like this, but I can't promise every date will be like this."

"I wouldn't expect it. This is… perfection."

He took her other hand, and stood facing her. "I couldn't agree more." He brushed soft his lips against hers. She pressed her lips against his, taking in both the smells of the ocean and of him. She could still smell his cologne after the long, elaborate day.

Zachary stepped back. "Will you teach me to dance some more? If my girlfriend," he looked hesitant, "is a dance instructor, I should know the basics, right?"

Her heart raced. "I couldn't agree more. The boyfriend," she grinned, "of a dance instructor really should know his stuff."

His face relaxed, and she pulled him toward her. "It's really about following your instincts."

"When it comes to dancing, I don't have any." He laughed, looking embarrassed. "I'm surprised your feet survived last time."

"Don't be silly. It just takes practice, and then your reservations will melt away."

Zachary didn't appear convinced.

"Think about writing," she said, sliding his arm to the small of her back. "You didn't wake up one day writing masterpieces, did you?"

"No, of course not. In fact, I haven't written one yet."

"I beg to differ," Jasmine said, "but that's not my point. You started writing stories as a boy, right?"

Zachary moved his legs, stepping on her right foot. "Sorry. See?"

She shook her head. "Not a problem. So, even something you're naturally gifted at has taken practice. This is no different."

Zachary looked down at his feet. "I suppose." He looked back up at her. "You know, I see what you're saying. Even before I started writing stories, I'd been telling them since I could speak."

"Exactly. That's like me with dancing. From what I've been told, I was dancing long before I even walked."

"How's that?" he asked.

"I would bust out moves while sitting whenever I heard music. My feet would kick even though they couldn't support my weight yet."

He laughed. "That's kind of how I feel now."

Jasmine shook her head. "Just follow my lead. I know it won't be long before I'm following yours."

"I wouldn't count on that."

"You have to drop your reservations and find your natural instincts. Once you do, you'll be golden."

"That's going to be easier said than done."

"And I think you're going to surprise yourself." She helped him glide along the sand to 'music' of the waves and birdsong. After a little while, he seemed to feel more comfortable—and step on her new shoes less. "See? You're already getting the hang of it."

"I wouldn't count on that."

"Oh, stop." They continued dancing around the shore. Watching him try so hard warmed her heart. She knew it was a challenge, just like trying to write a novel would be for her. But he was doing a lot better than she would at writing. Before long, he was moving with more confidence and grace.

He even got to the point where he stopped focusing on their feet and he looked up at her and danced, staring into her eyes.

Jasmine laced her fingers through his. "You're taking the training wheels off now," she whispered. "Soon you'll be learning the waltz."

"I doubt that. I'd just be happy to be able to take you to a dance and not step on your feet."

He leaned forward and pressed his lips against hers.

Twenty-Two

~

JASMINE HUNG THE DRESS IN her closet and slipped on her still-new pajamas, ready to fall asleep after a long, wonderful day.

Someone knocked on the door.

"Come in," she called, withholding a groan.

Lana entered, smiling. "How did your date go? You were gone *all* day." She looked Jasmine over. "And you look tanner, too."

Jasmine sighed dramatically. "It was the best—everything. He put so much thought into the date. I really don't know how he pulled it off. I know Rafael and Jake helped out with part of it."

Lana's eyes lit up. "Those Hunters are incredible, aren't they?"

Jasmine nodded. "That they are. I've never seen a family so dedicated to each other."

"Or so gorgeous." Lana fanned herself.

Jasmine laughed nervously.

"You know I'm right. I only have eyes for Brayden,

but there's no denying how beautiful they all are."

"I can't. Even though I did get the best looking one."

"We'll just have to agree to disagree." Lana sat down on Jasmine's bed. "So, tell me everything."

"This could take a while."

"I don't have anywhere to be." Lana leaned against the headboard, resting her hands behind her head.

"Okay." Jasmine sat at the end of the bed and started from the beginning and told her almost everything, leaving out some of the sweet words and kisses exchanged.

"That does sound like the perfect date. Did you talk to him about publishing his book online?"

"Before the date started, I brought it up. He wasn't very excited about it. Just said he was willing to wait as long as he needed to get the deal of his dreams."

Lana frowned. "I talked to Erin, and she said it's super easy to get started. The hard part is writing a good book, getting it edited, and marketing it."

"He already has that—well, the good book and the editing—but he doesn't want it as an ebook."

Lana leaned forward. "What if you surprised him by putting it up for him?"

Jasmine's stomach twisted in knots. "I don't think he'd like it."

"Not even if he sold enough to actually get a publisher's attention? According to Erin, they notice stuff like that, and if his book is as good as you say, they'll have to."

"But what if they don't?" Jasmine's mind raced. She would love to help Zachary reach his dreams, but she didn't want to risk making him mad, either. It was his book, his decision.

"Don't you think they will?" Lana asked. "You're the one who's read it."

Jasmine's palms sweated. "I don't know anything about publishing houses or ebook marketing."

"But we can talk to my cousin."

Jasmine's heart pounded in her chest. She shook her head, feeling sick. "I don't think I can."

"I'll talk to her," Lana said.

"That's not what I meant."

Lana's eyes lit up. "Imagine how thrilled Zachary will be to get a deal. Think of his smile."

Jasmine's mouth went dry. "I don't think it's a good idea. He'll feel better if he gets it himself."

"It's his book, right? You're not going to do anything to change it. It's all him, just a little bit of marketing help from you."

"I'd be going behind his back."

Lana frowned. "Not really. It's more like a surprise party. Sure, you have to sneak around and fib a little, but it's all for the greater good."

"I'm not so sure."

Lana patted Jasmine's knee. "Tell you what. Think

about it—sleep on it. We'll talk in the morning. I'm supposed to call Erin then, anyway. If you don't want to do this, I'll let her know. But if you do, then she can walk us through the process. Sound good?"

Jasmine's heart pounded so hard she swore Lana could hear it, too. "I'll sleep on it."

"And if you really think it's a bad idea, I won't bring it up again. I just can't help but think how happy you'll make him."

"Maybe."

"Okay." Lana stood, stretching. "It's late, anyhow. Probably not the best time for making big decisions. Have a good night."

"You, too." Jasmine turned out the lights and climbed into bed, her mind still racing. She loved the idea of helping Zachary sell his book, but he had seemed pretty certain about not going to ebooks first. But what if it was like dancing? What if he just needed to see what was possible first?

Jasmine closed her eyes, her mind racing. The last thing she wanted to do was go behind his back, and she wasn't sure it was like Lana had said. It didn't feel like planning a surprise party. This was Zachary's career—his dream. It was his book, and if he didn't want to put it out there without a publishing house, who was she to do it?

He was the best thing to have happened to her—ever. Zachary was better than landing the lead in the

Nutcracker. Granted, that had been in Delaware, but she had always wanted to dance that part on stage, and she had done it. She would give up dancing altogether if it meant she could be with him.

Never before had she met anyone who had gone to so much trouble to make her feel special.

Jasmine finally fell asleep, and she dreamed of Zachary and his novel all night long. In some dreams, she had uploaded his book and it had sold millions of copies, winning him deals he'd never thought of. In other dreams, she did the same and he ended up angry with her, yelling at her to leave Kittle Falls and never return.

She woke up twisted in the sheets, sweating. Never before had she been so conflicted over anything. She glanced over at the time, and saw that it was still early.

Her mind raced, and she felt like she had barely slept—it certainly hadn't been a restful sleep. She got up and looked out the window. It seemed darker than it should be, even though it was still early. Could the summer be winding down already? Time for the daylight hours to start lessening?

Looking up at the sky, she noticed clouds. Jasmine hadn't even thought they existed here in Kittle Falls. Maybe it was going to rain.

She hoped to stay longer and find out what the rest of the seasons were like.

Did she dare set up his book online? Lana would

want to know soon.

She felt like throwing up.

If he had been even slightly positive about the idea of ebooks, she would feel better about surprising him, but the look on his face the day before told her it wasn't a good idea. On the other hand, he would be thrilled to know that people loved his books.

She knew they would. That was why she hadn't been able to put down his novel, despite her lack of sleep and the other stresses in her life. It had been the ideal escape—the world that her boyfriend created had given her the perfect getaway.

Zachary deserved to be noticed. It seemed like the only way his future fans would find him would be without publishers. They wouldn't even read the best book ever written. How would they ever publish it, much less market it to thriller readers, if they wouldn't give him the chance he deserved?

His book could easily have its own table in the bookstores with all the other bestselling authors. Jasmine knew she was biased, but at the same time, she also knew he had written a great book. One that only needed a little push, and then it would explode in popularity. That much she knew with all of her heart.

Maybe Lana was right. Then he would adore her even more. Zachary might look at her with that beautiful smile, even wider and more gorgeous than she'd ever seen.

Smiling, Jasmine grabbed some clothes and went into the bathroom and took a shower. This was going to be a big day. Obviously, not the day she would tell him about putting his book out there. She would wait until it had sold so many books he would be shocked—impressed even, looking at her with more love and caring than before.

After she was ready, she went downstairs and found Lana's parents already eating breakfast.

"You must be an early riser," Dwight said, looking up from the Sunday paper.

"Sometimes." Jasmine smiled.

"Help yourself to some food," Susan said. "I made a breakfast casserole."

"Thank you," Jasmine said. "It smells delicious."

She took a small helping—she already had calories to burn after yesterday—and made small talk with them while they ate.

Jasmine went upstairs and ran into a very tired-looking Lana.

"Did you decide?" Lana asked, rubbing her eyes.

Pulse racing, Jasmine nodded. "I want to surprise him."

Lana's face lit up. "Oh, good. He's going to love you for this. Let me just get ready, and then we can call Erin."

"I can't wait." Jasmine went back into her room and made her bed, eager to get started with their plans.

She checked her phone to see if she'd missed any calls or texts. There was a message from the rental insurance. She held her breath, staring at the number. She couldn't bring herself to listen to the message. Today was going to be part of the overall flawless weekend. She couldn't risk finding out that she wouldn't be reimbursed for anything she'd lost.

First thing the next morning, she would listen. Then if it was bad news, she'd be able to call them back. Today, probably not. In fact, given that it was a Sunday, the message was probably automated. Either a general message saying she'd be covered, or more likely, a general message saying she hadn't. If she'd been covered, there would be a lot of details to go over. What details would be involved with saying no? Easy enough for just a message.

Jasmine pushed the thoughts out of her mind. Either way, she was no better or worse off than at that current moment.

Lana burst into the room, pulled out her phone, and slid her fingers around the screen. "Putting it on speaker."

Jasmine heard the phone ringing.

"Lana?"

"Hey, Erin. Thanks so much for your help." Lana smiled at Jasmine. "I've got Jasmine here. What do we need to do to get started?"

Twenty-Three

~

ZACHARY CLOSED HIS LAPTOP, SET it on the bed, and went into the living room. Rafael sat on the couch, smiling at his phone.

"Good news?" asked Zachary.

Rafael looked up. "What? Oh, yeah. I just got a message that I was approved for the retail space I want. The one next to the bridal shop. This is huge. People go to the wedding store to spend big bucks. They'll see my designer threads and want to buy them for their rehearsal dinners and honeymoon wear." Rafael was happier than Zachary had seen him since coming back into town.

"Congrats, Raf." Zachary sat next to him and read over the email. "You didn't think you'd get the space?"

Rafael shrugged. "Another guy was bidding for it, too, and he has a successful store not far away. I thought he might have a better chance because of that. Especially now that my name is off the company I started in LA." He shook his head. "Apparently, they did their homework and saw what I had built from nothing. They thought I would be a better fit for the strip mall."

"See? Things are starting to turn around," Zachary said. "And if you ever want to talk about what happened down in LA, just let me know. I'm still willing to let you vent."

Rafael's face clouded over. "Not sure I'll ever be ready to talk about that."

"I've always been able to keep your secrets. I never told anyone about the time you snuck the—"

"Got it. And I appreciate it. Hey, speaking of your trustworthiness, I'm going to need someone to help me getting all this stuff going. I know you need to write, but could you help me on the side until your books take off? It's going to take a lot of work to get my store running before I can even open."

"Can I start in a week? Mom and Dad already paid me an advance—which I've already spent."

"No problem. How long do you think you'll be able to stick around?"

"I'm not really sure at this point."

"What's going on with your book?" Rafael asked.

"My agent is still going after the publishing houses. Now she's sharing the proposal for the book I'm currently working on."

"She can do that? Even though it's not done?"

"Sure, if they like the idea, then I can send them a sample. But at the rate I'm going, it'll be done before anyone expresses any interest."

"What about self publishing? A lot of people in LA are into that. Some of them were doing pretty well with it."

Zachary scowled. "Why is everyone bringing that up?"

"People don't look down on it like they used to, you know. I've heard—"

"I'm not interested." Zachary folded his arms.

"Well, don't say I never tried to help." Rafael shook his head. "How'd your date with Jasmine go? It looked like it got off to a good start." He turned and gave Zachary his full attention.

"Yeah, it did. It only got better as the day went on. I showed her everything Kittle Falls has to offer."

"And she was still impressed?" Rafael laughed.

"She said she felt like a princess."

"So, is it serious?" Rafael slid his phone into a pocket.

"I think so. She didn't object when I called her my girlfriend."

"Nice." He glanced toward the window. "Good thing you took her out yesterday. Looks like it might rain today."

Zachary looked outside. "Those clouds do look menacing. I wonder if fall is going to make an early appearance this year."

"It might. I heard it's supposed to be a cold, snowy

winter."

"Really?" Zachary shivered just thinking about it. "I've never been a fan of the white stuff."

"No?" Rafael asked. "I love it. Maybe because I've missed it living down south."

"Could be. We had plenty in New York," Zachary said. "I could go the rest of my life without ever seeing another flake."

"Think about the snowmen you could build with Jasmine. And the snowball fights."

"You always did like snowball fights." Zachary frowned, remembering some of the many snowballs to the face his brother had thrown at him over the years.

Rafael laughed, obviously remembering the same thing. "Maybe she can teach you to duck," he teased.

"Ha, ha." Zachary checked the time. "I'd better get to the shop. It's going to be my second home this week."

"Then my shop will be. Right?"

"If I want to keep taking Jasmine out, it will be. The rest of this week is going to be filled with inexpensive dates. Tonight we're supposed to go to Jake and Tiffany's for dinner."

"How's Tiff feeling?" Rafael asked. "She didn't look so good last time."

"Jake thinks it's getting better."

"I'm sure she appreciates you being at the shop so she doesn't have to be."

"Anything for our first niece or nephew."

Zachary rose and went to the kitchen, grabbing his leftovers from the previous night—there was enough for three meals. He piled a little of this and that on his plate and stuck it in the microwave, and then ate it as fast as he could.

He received a text. Heart pounding, he checked, hoping it was Jasmine.

Nope. It was only Jake wanting to know if he was on his way.

Be there in a minute.

Zachary finished the last few bites and then rushed out the door. There was no time for walking—not that he wanted to with the chill in the air. It almost felt like it could snow that day, but he knew it wouldn't. Not before the fall even hit.

Hopefully, the cold weather wouldn't scare off the tourists. His family depended on the income from the whole summer to get them through the rest of the year. They still had business in the off season, but it didn't compare to the summer. Even though Kittle Falls used some of the holidays—like Halloween, Christmas, and Valentine's Day—to draw in visitors year round, nothing else compared to the business the warm months brought.

With any luck, Zachary would get a book deal and have so much money his parents wouldn't need to worry about finances anymore.

"There he is," Cruz said as Zachary walked through the shop doors. "I told you he'd be here."

"You doubted?" Zachary asked, shooting a playful glare at Jake.

"You *are* late."

"Less than five minutes." Zachary shook his head. "And the place is so busy, too." There wasn't a single customer in sight.

"That's because it's so cold," Jake said. "Hopefully, everyone won't stay inside today."

"I'm sure the clouds will blow away. What do you need me to do?" Zachary asked.

Cruz handed him a clipboard. "You can check the inventory. I did that last time."

"Hope I remember how to do it." Zachary took the clipboard.

"It ain't hard, yo. Count the items and write down the numbers."

Zachary walked over to the frozen foods and counted. Even though it was a tedious task, the time still went quickly.

Before he knew it, sounds of customers filled the shop. He peeked outside and saw that the sun was finally out. On days like this, it sucked that business relied so heavily on the weather. But then again, they'd only had a few rainy days all season, so there wasn't much to complain about—as long as the fall didn't arrive early.

Between helping customers find items and finishing the inventory, the day hurried by. Calvin and Bella arrived in the mid-afternoon, and Zachary finally was able to leave.

Perfect timing for him to get back home and change before meeting with Jasmine.

Before climbing into his car, he sent her a quick text.

Can't wait to see you. Still on for dinner?

Yeah. Wouldn't miss it. Should I meet you at your house again?

Sure. Half an hour work?

Perfect. Dancing hearts followed the message.

He sent her some kissing smilies and then got in the car. A half an hour would give him exactly the time he needed to get ready.

Zachary thought about the previous day's date the entire time he got ready, and he grew more excited to see Jasmine. It was hard to believe they had only known each other a short time. She'd worked her way into his heart and life like no one else had managed, and he'd thought that would be impossible after dealing with Monica. In fact, Jasmine had helped him nearly forget about his evil ex.

He'd been ready to write off relationships until he bumped into Jasmine. He would have to give Brayden a huge thank you gift for talking him into working out. Otherwise, he would've missed out on the best thing in his life—and he wouldn't have even known.

When he went out to the hallway, heading for the living room, he heard conversation. It sounded like Jasmine had already arrived. Zachary ran his hands through his hair to make sure the gel hadn't made it too stiff and then he rounded the corner to see Jasmine sitting with Rafael. He was showing her something on his phone.

"Zachary!" Jasmine jumped up and ran over to him, giving him a big hug. She nearly knocked him over.

"That's a greeting I could get used to." Zachary laughed, squeezing her tight.

"I missed you," she said.

"Me, too."

"Didn't you guys just see each other last night?" Rafael teased.

"It's too long to be apart," Jasmine said. "You wouldn't understand because you live with him. You can see him anytime you want."

Rafael laughed. "Right. That must be it."

"Makes me wish I could trade places with you," Jasmine said.

"No." Zachary shook his head.

"Why not?" Jasmine asked.

"Because if you were Rafael, I couldn't do this." He leaned in and kissed her soft lips, pressing firmly. She smelled of flowers and cinnamon.

"I can't argue with that."

"Are you ready?" he asked. "I thought we could walk along the boardwalk before going over to Jake and Tiffany's. When I left, Jake was still talking to customers, so I'm sure they're not ready for us just yet."

She took his hand. Her skin was so smooth and soft against his. It felt a little cooler than normal, though. Maybe she was cold because of the change in weather. It seemed to affect everyone, and that was all anyone seemed to talk about all day in the store. If they weren't asking where something was located, they spoke of the chilly weather.

"Have fun, you two," Rafael said, going back to his phone.

They went outside and walked toward the beach. Jasmine seemed happy, but didn't say much.

"Is everything okay?" Zachary asked.

"Yeah. Chilly, isn't it?" She shivered.

He put his arm around her. "Probably just a fluke. Would you rather not go to the boardwalk?"

"I don't mind." A breeze picked up and blew her hair in her face.

"Are you sure?" Zachary asked. "We can go into some stores or sit under a covered area."

"Maybe we could sit." She seemed distracted.

They went over to a covered area, usually used by those who wanted a break from the sun. They sat on a bench and watched the ocean waves from a distance. Birds flew around, some dipping down to catch fish.

"It's pretty," Jasmine said. "It's actually kind of a nice change."

Zachary pulled her closer. "And it gives me a good excuse to keep you warm."

She snuggled against him and took a deep breath. "I have a confession."

"What?" Zachary's heart dropped.

Twenty-Four

~

JASMINE'S PULSE RACED. SHE WANTED Zachary to say something, anything.

"What kind of a confession?" he finally asked.

She took his hand and squeezed it. "I almost put your book for sale as an ebook."

He jumped back, letting go of her. "You what?"

"Almost. I wanted you to see how popular it would become. I really believe in you and this is going to be a bestseller, Zachary. I hate that those publishers won't even look at it."

He stared at her, not saying anything. His mouth formed a straight line.

She swallowed. "I even talked with someone who told me how to do it. But in the end, I didn't do it. As much as I believe in you and your book, I didn't want to do anything behind your back—even if it would have earned you a huge following and thousands of sales."

Zachary continued staring, and his face didn't give any indication of what he thought. Except that he wasn't happy.

She took a deep breath. "And I didn't want any secrets between us, so I had to tell you—even though you probably never would have found out."

His face turned red, but he still didn't say anything.

Jasmine bit her lip. "I know you have a bestseller on your hands, but I respect your wishes too much."

Zachary stood, his fists clenched. His eyebrows came together. "I can't believe this."

A lump formed in her throat. "I didn't do it."

"Why would you even *think* about it?" he asked, his voice rising with each word.

Tears stung her eyes. "I didn't have to tell you."

"I told you how I felt about it."

"But I thought it would be a nice surprise. Then I came to my senses and knew what the right thing to do was. That's what I did."

Zachary shook his head and stepped back. "I need some space."

"But, Zachary—"

"I'm sorry, Jasmine. Our date today isn't going to work, after all."

She opened her mouth, but closed it. "If that's the way you feel."

He nodded and then pulled out his phone and slid his finger around the screen. "Jake? ... Sorry to cancel at the last minute, but Jasmine and I won't be able to make it. ... Oh, she's not? ... I suppose everything

works out, then. Tell Tiffany I hope she feels better. ….
Yeah, bye."

Jasmine stared at him, her vision growing blurry
tears. "I'm sorry, Zachary."

"I just need some space. I need to think—to process
everything."

"Okay." Jasmine stayed in her seat while Zachary
walked away. She'd always thought honesty was the best
policy, but maybe not. That wasn't how she'd expected
him to react. He was supposed to appreciate her honesty.

Tears fell to her face. She was supposed to tell him,
and then he was supposed to realize how much she cared
for and believed in him. Then at least consider the idea
of publishing straight to readers. To at least give her the
benefit of the doubt.

She sat and let the tears fall for a minute before the
sadness left and she the familiar feeling of anger started
to replace it. It started in the pit of her stomach until it
reached her chest, and she was ready to yell and throw
things.

Just like her parents. She froze. Acting like them was
unacceptable.

Then she thought back to Zachary's unjustified response. How dare he be mad at her? Jasmine was only
trying to help, and she didn't have to be honest with
him. She *could* have easily decided not to upload the file
and be done with it. But she wanted to start off their

relationship with transparency.

So much for that. Now she'd probably lost his trust—all when trying to do the right thing.

Maybe her mom *was* right, and no one was actually trustworthy. She'd always told Jasmine that the only person she could count on was herself, and especially not some man. But after seeing everything her parents went through—and put her through—she desperately wanted to believe the opposite was true. That someday she would find someone who trusted and loved her wholeheartedly. And she'd thought she'd found that in Zachary.

She'd had in her mind that she could return home one day, show him off, and prove them all wrong. Prove that if she fought hard enough, she could move past everything they had ever taught her and tried to instill in her.

That could have been a foolish choice. What if they'd been right all along? But even if they had, their life wasn't the one she wanted. She couldn't give up hope. Jasmine wanted to live exactly the opposite of them. Not only for herself, but also for Carter.

She got up and looked around, not seeing Zachary anywhere. He was already out of sight.

Part of her wanted to let him have it—and not space—while the other part of her thought it was maybe for the best. If she ran after him and tried to force her opinion on him, was she any better than her parents who screamed at each other for hours on end? Neither ever managed to win the other over, and when they did yell, eventually someone ended up with a bruise or a gash.

No. She needed to give Zachary the space he needed. If she learned anything from her parents all those years, it was how *not* to treat someone.

If he couldn't accept her honesty, then it just wasn't meant to be. No matter how much it broke her heart. She wasn't going lie and hide things to keep the peace. Yes, she wanted peace and happiness, but not at the expense of harboring secrets.

Jasmine went out from the covered area and the wind blew her hair around. Rain picked up and whipped around her, hitting her in the face. Pulling her hair away, she looked around again, still not seeing him.

She made her way back to Lana's house. Her car would be fine in front of the Hunter's house, and besides, Lana's house was closer to the boardwalk.

Jasmine went inside and typed in the code for the security system.

"Back so soon?" asked Dwight, looking up from his papers.

"It didn't work out for today," Jasmine said. She forced a smile, hoping he wouldn't ask any questions.

"That's too bad. Feel free to watch the TV if you want. It won't disturb me."

"Thanks. Maybe later." Jasmine headed upstairs,

trying to shake off the negative feelings. There was too much of that in her life already. She didn't need more. If it didn't work out with Zachary, she would just go back to Portland, work wherever she could, and focus on her dancing. Just like she'd been planning all along.

She might even open her own dance studio. Spending time with the Hunters must have been rubbing off on her—they were pretty much all making their own destinies. Brayden with his clinic, Cruz with his tattoo parlor, Rafael with his fashion store, Jake buying his parents' shop, and of course Zachary with his writing—even if he was stubborn and rash.

Jasmine reclined on the bed, thinking about the possibilities of her own studio. If she worked for a while, that would save money. She'd be out of school and not traveling, so if she had a roommate or two, that would cut her expenses even further.

It would also give her a decent savings, and if she worked for a while, that would show the banks that she had a consistent income and would be able to pay off any loans she needed. Returning to Portland would be a good location—it was far away from her parents and Kittle Falls.

She already knew enough people that it wouldn't be starting over like she'd been doing the whole time she'd been traveling to dance. There were already ten people she had in mind who might possibly room with her.

The more she thought about it, the more excited she

became. Her own dance studio. No, it wouldn't be like working at one of the prestigious ones, but she could run things the way she wanted. The entire studio would be hers for the designing. She would set the hours and maybe even hire people to work for *her*.

She might even have a class for the low income—knowing herself how hard it was for kids who wanted to start dancing early, but couldn't because their parents wouldn't get a job. She'd love to give kids a chance she would have jumped at, and maybe even teach them life skills they wouldn't get elsewhere.

Jasmine's excitement grew. It would be possible to start her studio where it would be more accessible to the inner city kids and the trailer parks and low-income housing. Maybe even hire some teens to help with those classes for the poor kids so that she could help even more kids.

She sat up and grabbed her phone, searching to see what was available in those areas. There was plenty of retail space, none that had been a dance studio, so she would definitely need a loan to get it set up.

Jasmine looked for dance studios with openings for teachers, and none of the ones she wanted had openings listed. They had probably offered their spots to the interns. That wouldn't stop her from asking, but she needed to look for other studios. If she needed to room with five other girls, sleep on a bunk bed, and work at a lower paying job, she would if that was what it would take.

Opening a studio would take sacrifice—maybe a lot of it—but it would be worth it in the end, when she had her own studio and help kids with as few opportunities as she'd had.

There was a knock on her door.

"Come in."

Lana came in. "Dad said you were here. What's going on? I thought you were supposed to eat at Jake and Tiffany's."

"She wasn't feeling well."

Lana sat down, watching Jasmine. "Nothing else is wrong?"

Jasmine shrugged. "I'm just looking at possibilities for opening a dance studio. I really want my own, even if it takes years of saving."

"That's not what I asked."

Jasmine turned the screen off and put her phone on the night stand. She looked at Lana. "I told Zachary about almost putting his book up online."

"And?"

"Let me put it this way. It's a good thing we never actually did it, given how mad he is at me for considering it."

Lana frowned. "What? That doesn't sound like him."

Jasmine didn't say anything. Apparently it was like him—because it was him.

"But if it sold thousands of—"

"It was just a bad idea," Jasmine said. "I was right to leave the decision up to him. It's his story, and if he wants to waste years waiting for a company to publish it, that's his choice."

"Why did you tell him?" Lana asked. "I mean, you didn't even do it."

"I'd hoped he'd be excited about how much I believed in him, but that backfired." She rested her chin on her knees.

"I'm sure he'll come around," Lana said. "He adores you."

Jasmine frowned. "He was pretty mad. If he feels like he can't trust me, I can't blame him. I should have respected his wishes to begin with."

"This is my fault," Lana said. "I'm the one who pressured you into this. I'm really sorry. I'll talk to him."

"No. That might make things worse. Let him stew, and then if he wants to talk to me, great. If not, then it wasn't meant to be."

Lana's eyes widened. "How can you say that? You guys are perfect for each other."

"Face the facts, Lana. Everything has been a whirlwind with us." Jasmine sighed. "I've been high on emotion with my mother showing up and my condo burning down. His emotions have been elevated, too, finally facing how he feels about the death of Sophia. Maybe we were just meant to be here to help each other through some tough times. Now it's time to move on and go in different directions."

"How can you even think like that?" Lana asked. "I'm going to talk to him."

"Please just let it be. Whatever happens, happens. I don't feel like fighting destiny."

Twenty-Five

~

ZACHARY SLAMMED THE FRONT DOOR so hard the walls shook. He put his hand out to steady a picture of his family from when he was about ten years old.

"No slamming doors" called his dad.

"Sorry," Zachary said, though he held no remorse. He went down the hall and into his room. He wanted to slam that door, too, but wanted everyone to leave him alone even more, so he didn't.

What Zachary needed was to throw his emotions into his writing. He knew himself well enough to know he wouldn't be able to process anything without writing something down. He'd have to take it out on his novel.

Damion hadn't had enough drama, and now Zachary had more than enough passion to throw at him. Either the readers would hate Zachary for being so mean to Damion, or they would love the suspense.

Zachary didn't care either way. If it ended up being a horrible scene, he could delete it. He'd been writing so much lately, anyway. Throwing out a chapter or two wouldn't be a huge deal. At least he would probably feel better.

He read the last few lines he'd written to get back into the story and then started typing. An antagonist that had only been mentioned up until this point showed up, surprising Damion on his quest.

Zachary's fingers flew faster than ever before. He made more typos than before, also, but he didn't care. That stuff could be fixed later. At the rate his agent and the publishing houses moved, he could do the draft over ten times before anyone ever saw it.

He threw all of his frustrations at his characters, making their lives ten times more miserable than his was. Zachary even threw in some relationship problems so he could feel better about his own life. At least now his life was better than someone's, even if it was a fictional person.

A knock sounded at the door.

"Go away." Zachary didn't slow his typing.

The door opened, anyway. Rafael came in. "What's going on?"

"I'm *trying* to write." Zachary didn't look up from his laptop.

"That's not what I mean."

"It's what I mean." Zachary continued pounding on the keys, hoping his brother would get a clue.

"Why'd you slam the door?"

"I need to get this done, Raf."

"Why? Got a publishing deadline?"

Zachary straightened his back, and shot his brother an angry stare.

"At least I got you to pay attention to me," Rafael said. "What's going on? Why aren't you with Jasmine?"

"I don't want to talk about it." He turned back to his computer screen.

"Too bad, little brother. I can still beat you up, so talk to me."

"No you can't."

"Want me to try?" Rafael asked, unbuttoning the cuff of his silk sleeve. "I still work out every day. Haven't stopped."

"I'm taller now, *big* brother."

"By an inch?" Rafael asked, not looking impressed. "Talk to me, or we'll take it outside."

"Why should I talk to you?" Zachary demanded, his anger rising. "You haven't told me anything about why you left LA. I've asked you multiple times, and you stonewall me. I'm just returning the favor. Now leave me alone." He glared at his brother.

"Is that what you think? I just don't want to talk to you?"

"What else? We used to be close, but now we're not. That's fine. We haven't talked much over the last few years. Whatever. Let me write."

"Did the big apple turn you into a punk?" Rafael asked.

Zachary narrowed his eyes. "Go. Away."

"You really want me to tell you what happened?" asked Rafael.

"I don't care anymore."

"Whatever." Rafael sat on the twin bed, forcing Zachary to move over.

He backed up his document and then put his laptop on the desk. "You have my attention. Now talk."

"Only if you agree to tell me what's going on."

"We'll see."

Rafael took a deep breath. "Fine. Here's the deal. There were a couple big things that happened all at once. Not only that, but some smaller things had been growing, making me eager to leave. But I stuck it out because I had my business and my girlfriend."

"I knew all that," Zachary said. "Mostly."

Rafael leaned against the headboard, kicking his feet onto the bed. "First of all, my business partner made some decisions without talking with me. Some partner, huh? He made deals we had no way of being able to follow through on. He promised a large company a huge order that would take twice our staff to complete, and he gave them a stupid discount to top it off."

"Back stabbed. I know how that feels."

Rafael raised an eyebrow. "Anyway, he swore we could do it and that it would bring in more money in the long run because the other company would continue business with us. We lost half of what we had built and saved—over that one stupid deal. We barely remained in the black. I had never lost so much sleep in my life. Not just worrying about everything, but having to spend every waking hour working on fulfilling that order. And no, the other company didn't come back to us with business. Long story short, the mess trickled down and affected our other accounts."

Rafael paused, looking deep in thought. "If I'd have been smart, I would have kicked him out of the business. It was my business. I had been the one to start it up and get it off the ground. He'd joined to help expand it. Instead, he nearly killed it. In trying to fix that mistake, he made a bunch of other really stupid business decisions. Then we did end up in the red. He destroyed everything I'd built."

"That sucks."

"It more than sucks, and it's not even the end of it. I wanted him to leave, but he wouldn't. I couldn't get rid of him, so I walked away from the business that had been not only my lifelong dream, but my blood, sweat, and tears. He had nothing to buy me out with, so I just signed it over to him, not wanting to be in charge of all that debt. It was as clean of a break as I could manage."

Suddenly, Zachary understood his brother's recent broodiness. "Sorry about all that."

"You think that's the end of my story?" Rafael asked.

"Uh, I guess not."

"Not only did Tony mess me over by ruining my business, but then I found out he'd been seeing Kristine behind my back the entire time, too. The two of them took such pleasure in ruining my life and dream. Now they run my business together." Anger clouded his face. "Betrayed by a friend and the one I thought was the love of my life. That's why I'm starting over this time on my own. No business partner—unless you count Mom and Dad, but they're not going to do anything to hurt me, and I'm going to pay them back."

"Not going to see anyone, either?" Zachary asked.

"Nope. My focus is going to be on the business and nothing else. I'm not letting anyone close enough to hurt me again, but I'm going to be so busy working it won't matter. I won't have time to miss romance and love. If I get lonely, I'll get a dog. Or just come over here for dinner more often."

"Wow, a dog or your family. Glad you think so highly of us." Zachary gave him a playful shove.

"You know I won't get a dog. They're too much work."

"They are cute, though. And loyal."

"I think I'll just focus on my business. So, now will you tell me what's eating you?" Rafael stared at him.

Zachary frowned. "I suppose I have to now. Everything was going so well with Jasmine, you know?"

Rafael nodded.

"Turns out she was going to load my novel to sell as

an ebook."

"And?"

"What do you mean 'and'? And everything. I don't want it as an ebook. It's my story, and she has no right. You want to talk about blood, sweat, and tears? I've poured my soul into it, only to have everyone in New York City reject it without even reading it. Now I have to write a second one, adding in elements I didn't really want, just so it will sell."

Rafael sat up straight. "Let me see if I understand this correctly. You're angry with her for something she didn't do?"

"What?" Zachary asked, confused.

"Jasmine didn't upload it, right?"

"She was *going to.*"

"And I assume you know that because she fessed up. No one came to you behind her back, right?" Rafael asked.

"What's your point?" Zachary narrowed his eyes.

"That you have a real winner."

"Pardon me?" Zachary asked.

"She believes in your story enough to do that for you."

"But she went behind my back to do it."

"And she didn't, right? She changed her mind and did the right thing."

Zachary frowned. "When you say it like that, you make me sound like a jerk."

"Just pointing out facts about her. She not only re-spected your wishes, but let you know what she almost did, even though she didn't have to."

"What exactly are you saying?" Zachary asked.

"Maybe you owe her an apology. It's not like she was seeing your best friend behind your back. She was trying to improve your career."

"I can do that myself, Rafael." Zachary folded his arms.

"Did you ever stop to think maybe she knows a thing or two about the ebook business?"

"Like what? She's a dancer. Not a writer, not a pub-lisher."

"And I'm a fashion designer, but I know that ebooks are where the industry is moving."

"Oh, really?" Zachary asked.

"You're so busy writing, you haven't paid attention to the changing publishing industry, have you?" Rafael asked.

"That's what my agent is for. And what do you know about book publishing?"

"I've had people tell me I need to write a book—lots of people. Everyone who's successful in their industry is writing a book these days. And most of them are skipping the agents and publishers."

"What good would writing a book do *you*?" Zachary asked.

"It's a way to get people in. They read your book—

see you as an authority in the field, and then want to go into business with you. In my case, purchase my clothing. I suppose if I'd listened to the advice and published a book, I might have had enough clients to make up for the damage Tony caused."

"I don't have anything to up-sell," Zachary said. "Publishing an ebook doesn't make sense. I want my books physically sitting in stores. Not on some virtual bookshelf."

"You can have both, you know."

"Maybe I don't *want* both."

"So, you just want to turn away money?" Rafael countered. "Not to mention that publishers also produce ebooks. And are you going to push away an amazing and beautiful woman, too? Are you going to keep working in the family shop for the next decade, also?"

Zachary frowned. "Publishers won't look at me if I self publish. It will kill my career."

"And who told you that?" Rafael asked. "Someone in traditional publishing?

"Your point?" Zachary's nostrils flared.

"Have you even studied the market?"

"I suppose you have." Zachary clenched his fists, not wanting to take his anger out on his brother.

"Some. After having enough people suggest I write a book, I did do a little research. Enough to know that publishers go after authors who prove themselves."

Zachary narrowed his eyes. He couldn't argue without looking into it himself, and he figured that between what Rafael and Jasmine had said, they were both probably right. And that meant his agent had been lying to him.

"It doesn't mean anything even if you're right, Rafael. The fact of the matter is that she took the file I gave her to read on her own and almost sold it."

"For you. To improve your career." Rafael stared at Zachary. "She believes in you. And even more importantly, she respects your feelings enough to not do what would help you—because you're hard-headed."

"Shut up."

"You'd better figure this out before she goes back to wherever she came from."

Twenty-Six

〜

JASMINE'S ALARM WENT OFF, BUT she barely heard it. She'd spent most of the night tossing and turning, half-hoping that Zachary would call her and half-planning her new studio in or near Portland. The best she could figure was that it would take two years to get it going. The worst case, five years. Either way was fine by her. She was willing to make the necessary sacrifices, and it would be well worth the wait.

On the other hand, she also wanted to spend more time with Zachary, and she would have gladly stayed in Kittle Falls to spend time with him—so long as he apologized for getting so angry with her. She would even travel to New York with him if he was that focused on getting a publishing deal. But if he couldn't understand her point of view, then she was more than willing to cut her losses and move on. She'd had enough heartbreak in her life to know she could heal and keep going.

She forced herself out of bed and got ready, nearly

falling asleep in the shower. "Pull yourself together. Those girls need you to focus," she muttered.

Once out, she pulled her hair back into a simple bun and applied minimal makeup—not that she was one to put on a lot, anyway. She threw a hoodie on over her dance wear and made it out of the house with little more than a casual greeting to Dwight.

It was dark, cold, and windy outside. What had happened to the nice weather they'd had all summer? Could the weather be sympathizing with her?

Jasmine looked down the street to figure out where she'd parked, but couldn't her car. Then she remembered—she'd left it across from the Hunter's house.

She wasn't going back for it now, and not only because of the weather—it was closer to the gym than to their house—but mostly because she didn't want to risk running into Zachary. Or any of his brothers. She didn't feel like trying to explain anything to them. They would all take his side.

Jasmine pulled the hoodie up over her bun, as close to her face as possible, and tightened the strings. The wind was growing stronger, and she didn't have much else to protect herself. She looked down toward the ground and jogged to the club, not bothering to stop for coffee, despite how cold and tired she was—with any luck the jog would be enough to wake her up.

It seemed to work. Once she got there, she felt fairly awake. More than she had back at the house, anyway.

"Hey, Jas!"

She turned around to see Kate. "Hey. How are you doing?"

"Pretty good, considering. Did you get your money from the insurance already?"

She'd forgotten she needed to call them back. "No. Did you?"

Kate shook her head. "I just barely sent out the paperwork." She gave Jasmine a once-over. "Where'd you get the new threads?"

Jasmine glanced down at her new clothes. "Oh, the family I'm staying with wanted to help me out."

"Nice. I should have stayed with you instead." Kate grinned.

"Ha, ha. Yeah. They're nice, but I want to find a way to pay them back somehow. I'm not really sure how, though."

"Do they want dance lessons?" Kate asked.

Jasmine tried to imagine Dwight doing ballet and smiled. "No, I can't picture that."

"Oh, I'm sure you'll think of something. Hey, girl. What about our double date?"

Her heart sank. "I forgot about that. Can I text you later?"

"Sure. Better get to my class. Want to hang out for lunch?" Kate asked. "I miss seeing you."

"Me, too. Lunch would be great." Especially since Jasmine had forgotten to pack anything. "Meet you in the employee lounge?"

Kate nodded and then headed down the hall.

The morning went surprisingly fast. Jasmine had a handful of new girls, but was surprised at how many returning faces she saw. All the regulars greeted her with big hugs and stories about what they did over the weekend. Most of them had seen the baby monkey riding on the pig. According to several of them, the pig had broken out of its area and ran all over the beach for nearly an hour—if she could trust first and second graders' estimation of time passing.

They all laughed about the pig and then got down to business. Some of the new girls had trouble with the moves, so Jasmine had the returning students help them out. It worked out well, and the girls teaching seemed really proud of themselves.

By the time lunch rolled around, Jasmine was famished and very much looking forward to eating with Kate. Not only would she get to eat for the first time that day, but Kate would be happy to talk the entire time, allowing Jasmine to sit quietly.

She grabbed her hoodie and made her way to the lounge, finding Kate chatting with a cute guy with bulging muscles. Jasmine stood by the door, waiting for Kate to finish flirting. Kate held up her pointer finger, letting Jasmine know it would only be a minute.

Jasmine went over to the coffee machine and poured herself a cup, emptying a couple single flavored creamer containers in. She drank the sweet caffeinated goodness while Kate flirted. Finally, Kate pulled herself away from the guy and joined Jasmine.

"Sorry about that. I've been trying to get Kevin's attention for ages. Turns out he just broke up with his girlfriend. Maybe he'll be the one who joins us on our date." Kate sighed, looking lost in thought.

"I'm starving. Let's go." Jasmine threw her empty cup in the garbage and pulled Kate out of the lounge. They went down the hall and turned a corner. Jasmine stopped cold.

"Jasmine," said Zachary.

"Zachary."

They stared at each other, neither speaking.

Kate extended her hand toward Zachary. "Kate." She smiled, oblivious to the tension.

Zachary turned to Kate and shook her hand. "Nice to meet you. Sorry I can't stay and talk, but I'm meeting my brother. And I'm already late."

"Maybe we'll meet again." Kate turned to Jasmine as Zachary walked away. "Who was that? The tension was so thick, it nearly strangled me."

Apparently she hadn't been oblivious, after all. Jasmine shook her head. "Let's just get lunch. We can talk then."

"Wait. He's not the guy…?"

A jumbled mixture of emotions rose up in Jasmine. She wasn't sure if she wanted to cry or yell, but after the way he had just acted, she leaned toward the latter.

"He's hot," Kate said. "What happened between the two of you?"

"I said we'll talk over lunch."

"So, he *is* the guy." Kate opened the doors outside, and a gust of wind nearly blew them back in. "Your car or mine?"

"Yours."

They ran to her car, and Jasmine managed to deflect every one of her questions until they sat down in a deli with their sandwiches.

"Okay, girlfriend," Kate said. "We're eating lunch, now spill it. You promised."

Jasmine sighed. "Yes, Zachary is the guy I was so excited about. Not so much now—obviously."

Kate sipped her drink. "What happened?"

"Maybe it's not meant to be."

"That doesn't tell me anything."

"People have differences of opinions, and sometimes those opinions are important enough that it won't work out." Jasmine took a large bite of her sandwich, hoping the need to chew would keep her from talking for a minute.

Kate frowned. "Guess I don't usually let it get that serious. Sorry you're having a hard time. Anything I can do?"

Jasmine shook her head, swallowing. "Either it's meant to be or it's not."

"What do you want?" Kate asked.

"I thought we really had a good thing going, you know?"

"Yeah," Kate said, "you were totally excited about him. And I can see why. I could stare him all day."

"It's more than just looks," Jasmine said.

"But looks play into it, right?" Kate smiled.

"Well, yeah, but they can't save a relationship, and that's not why I love him—I mean… why we grew close." Jasmine's face burned.

"Love?" Kate asked, staring at her.

"I didn't mean that, I meant—"

"But that's what you *said*." Kate's eyes were wide. "You said love."

"Not so loud."

"Do you?" Kate asked, lowering her voice.

Jasmine's eyes grew blurry with tears. "I thought so."

"Aw, sweetie." Kate patted Jasmine's hand. "If you do, we have something to fight for. Either you do or you don't. What is it? Is he worth fighting for? Do you love him?"

Jasmine wiped at her eyes. She nodded.

"Then we have to figure out how to win that hottie back. What do you think it'll take?"

"I don't know." Jasmine wiped at her eyes some more, but the tears wouldn't stop. Admitting how she felt hadn't helped anything—not if she wanted to keep herself together. "I don't really want to talk about it now, Kate."

"But if he means that much to you, we have to do something."

"What if I don't want to?" Jasmine asked, blinking more tears onto her face.

"Then I'd say you're lying."

"I'm not. He said he needs space to think about some things, and I'm giving it to him."

"Think he'd listen to me?" Kate asked.

"Probably not."

"So that's a maybe?" Kate looked at her hopefully.

"What are the chances of you running into him? He's probably already left the gym."

Kate pulled out her phone. "Nah. I'll bet he's still there. Guys always work out for at least an hour— usually longer if they have a workout buddy. They want to show off. It's kind of funny to watch, actually."

"That doesn't sound like Zachary. He's—"

"Every guy is like that," Kate said. "They're all competitive."

"Maybe just when they see you watching," Jasmine snapped. "Did you ever think of that?"

"No, but you make a good point. They don't want to look dumb if a pretty girl is watching." She paused. "Oh, come on. Not even a smile?"

Jasmine sighed.

"You're really upset about that guy. Dang." Kate gave her a sympathetic look.

Twenty-Seven

~

ZACHARY PUT THE LAST WEIGHT back and stretched his arms, glad to workout without the soreness he'd had before.

"Have you thought anymore about what I said earlier?" Brayden asked.

"I appreciate Lana taking responsibility," Zachary said, "but the fact is, Jasmine knew how I felt, and she was going to do it, anyway."

Brayden stared into his eyes, stepping closer. Usually, Zachary forgot about him being so much taller, but times like this, he couldn't.

"She didn't do it, though, did she?" Brayden asked, practically standing over Zachary. "She made the right choice in the end."

"I'm not going to be bullied into changing my mind."

Brayden stepped back. "I'm not bullying you. But I really think you should reconsider. Lana feels horrible and Jasmine—"

"So, really this is about Lana feeling bad." Zachary narrowed his eyes. "I'm supposed to overlook what Jasmine did so it'll make your fiancée feel better."

"That's not it, and you know it." Brayden frowned.

"Then just let me deal with this. I'm not mad at Lana."

"Jasmine really cares about you, Zachary. That much is obvious. She just wants to see you succeed."

"And she thinks she has to go behind my back to make that happen."

"Wouldn't you rather be with someone who believes in you than someone who doesn't?" Brayden narrowed his eyes.

Zachary knew he referred to Monica. "Yes, but not the way Jasmine went about it."

"She didn't do anything!" Brayden looked more frustrated than Zachary had seen him in a long time.

"Didn't do anything?" Zachary clenched his fists. "Look. We're done discussing this."

"You're being a jerk, you know that?"

Zachary stared at him. "Excuse me?"

"You heard me. Jasmine thought about doing something to help you, but then *didn't* because she knew how you felt about it."

"I don't need her help." His nostrils flared.

Brayden's lips curved down. "Don't let your pride get in the way of something as good as Jasmine. You won't find another like her anytime soon. Just think about all she's done for you in the short time you've known her."

Zachary opened his mouth, but nothing came.

"You know she cares about you, and you shouldn't treat her carelessly. You want space to think about what happened? Fine, but don't expect sympathy from me after you realize too late what you lost."

Zachary flung open his locker and threw the bag over his shoulder. "I don't need this from you. You're supposed to be on my side."

"Sometimes you need tough love."

"I have to get back to the shop." Zachary marched out into the hall.

"Oh, it's you again."

Zachary turned to see Jasmine's friend standing there. "I have to get to work."

"I don't know what happened between the two of you, but I can tell you one thing." She stepped closer, staring him down. "That girl cares about you—deeply. Whatever happened has hurt her a lot. I hope you guys can work it out because I've never seen her like this before."

He froze. Wait. He'd hurt her?

"Well, something to think about while you're on your way to work." She narrowed her eyes. "You know where to find Jasmine. Hopefully we can have that double date we've been talking about." She turned and walked away.

What was this? Make Zachary feel bad day? Everyone was on his case—was he really that far off? Jasmine had come super close to destroying his dreams. Self publishing would be the death of him getting a publishing deal.

But on the other hand, if what Rafael had said was true, then going the ebook route *might* not be such a bad idea—as long as it didn't ruin his chances of seeing his book sitting near the entrance of every major bookstore one day.

He sighed, lost in thought. When he got outside, the wind gave him a chill after working up a sweat in the gym. He readjusted his bag and then jogged over to the family shop to finish the week's work that he'd already been paid for.

That reminded him of his date with Jasmine—he'd used every last penny on her, and enjoyed it so much. They'd had so much fun that day. It had easily been one of the best days of his life... but then the next day. He frowned.

Maybe he had been rash... and rude.

Zachary opened the door to the shop, glad to step inside away from the wind. Cruz and Jake greeted him.

"You all right, dude?" Cruz asked.

"I think I blew it with Jasmine." He frowned.

"She'll forgive you, yo."

A group of customers came in, all running for the machine that dispensed warm drinks.

Cruz looked at Zachary. "We've got some new inventory to stock. Do you want to do that or man the register with Jake?"

He didn't feel like dealing with people. "I'll stock."

Zachary went into the back room and saw a stack of boxes nowhere near as big as the other day. With just him working on it, it could take hours, and with any luck, he wouldn't have to talk with anyone.

He took the first box and opened it, finding a variety of ramen noodles. He carried it back to that area of the store, finding that it had arrived just in time. Apparently with the cold weather, it was a popular item.

It was a good thing they sold more than just ice cream, or they'd be hurting now with the unseasonably cold weather.

Zachary stocked box after box, trying not to think of Jasmine, but she kept entering his mind. Not just her pretty face, but also her laugh and all the fun times they had. He couldn't stop thinking about their last date, the one where she had claimed to feel like a princess. Did she now feel a pauper?

He grimaced. More than likely, especially with the cold shoulder he'd given her at the gym. Guilt stung at him. He'd been unreasonable—all he'd been able to see was that she had almost destroyed everything he'd worked so hard for, and on purpose even.

But maybe that wasn't the case, and the more he thought about it, he realized it probably wasn't.

Zachary thought back to the day when she had gone with him to Sophia's grave. Jasmine had barely known him, but they'd really connected, having both lost siblings. She most certainly didn't have to go with him, but she did, and she'd been so kind and patient, allowing him to grieve.

He hung his head, feeling like a jerk. Brayden and Rafael had been right—that was exactly what he was being. Jasmine was a rare find, and he had quite possibly blown it. He needed to make things right. Now.

Zachary flattened the empty box next to him and went to the register. "I'm going to take a break."

Jake and Cruz waved him off, busy with customers. Zachary went into the back room and put the box away. He sat on a stool and called Jasmine. It went to voice mail. He hesitated, but ended the call. She would see that he called. He didn't want to leave his apology on a message.

He went to his browser app and searched what he could find on self publishing versus traditional publishing. There were a lot of sources claiming everything that Rafael had said.

It was enough to give him second thoughts, especially if it wasn't going to ruin his chances with the publishing houses. There were an impressive number of successful authors claiming they'd been approached by publishing companies after finding success online.

Zachary called Jasmine again. It went to voice mail

again, and he wondered if she was avoiding his calls—not that he could blame her—he needed to plead his case at least a little.

"Hi Jasmine. We need to talk... well, more accurately, I need to apologize. I hope you'll hear me out." He paused and then ended the call.

He looked at the clock. It was time to get back to work, but he wasn't ready. He called his agent.

"Zachary Hunter," she bellowed. "How's California treating you?"

"Good. Hey, Janice. I've got the next book almost ready. It has a healthy dose of romance, just like you said. When can we get it ready to send out?"

"Let me check my schedule." He heard papers shuffling on the other end of the phone followed by the clicking of computer keys. "I'm booked until spring."

"Spring?" Zachary exclaimed. "That's nearly a year away."

"I know, darling, but you went off the grid."

"It's the twenty-first century, Janice. It shouldn't matter if I live in Antarctica. We have phones and email. You can—"

"Want me to book you for May, darling?"

Zachary made a fist. "Why are you doing this to me? You said my series would sell."

"It hasn't, but I have a good feeling about May."

"I wrote the story with all the elements you suggested."

"Perfect. Send it to the editor and we'll go full force in the spring."

"That's unacceptable."

"It's going to have to work, darling."

"Don't call me that. You do realize I could publish them on my own?"

"And you'll ruin your career. I guarantee it. The publishing houses will never touch you again."

"That's a lie," Zachary said through gritted teeth. "And I'm done getting the runaround from you. When they come to me with a deal, don't expect a call from me."

"What? Wait, Zachary."

"No. I'm done. I could publish my whole series before you get one person to even look at any of them. My time is more valuable than that. Unless you can push me up in your calendar, we have nothing else to discuss."

"Well, I never—"

"That's right. You never did anything to help me, and you're not going to in the future, either. Goodbye, Janice." He ended the call, wishing his parents had a punching bag in the back room. Not only had he gotten the runaround from his agent, but she'd lied to him about the changing industry.

It was his fault for not doing his own research. He shouldn't have blindly accepted everything she said.

His phone rang, and he checked it, hoping it was Jasmine. It was Janice. He rejected the call and then went into his contacts list and blocked her. He stuffed the phone into his pocket and clocked out. He made a mental note to send her a letter of termination later.

Fuming, he went out to the shop. Jake was ringing up a customer, but Cruz was free.

"Whoa, dude. What's up?"

"I need to take the rest of the day off," Zachary seethed. "I'll work an extra day if I have to, but I can't be here right now."

"Sure, man. Whatever. If you need anything, let me know."

Zachary nodded and then headed outside. The sun had come out, but it was still windy.

He wanted to talk with Jasmine, but first he had some energy to burn off, and he needed the punching bag to do that.

Twenty-Eight

~

JASMINE WAVED GOODBYE TO THE last girls leaving for the day. She wasn't sure how she'd managed to make it through the afternoon after talking with Kate. She'd been an emotional wreck since accidentally saying that she loved Zachary.

Did she really? Had it been a Freudian slip? She didn't know, and she didn't want to think about it. It hurt too much, and she didn't want any more pain in her life. If Zachary didn't want her in his life, then she would let him walk away, no hard feelings. She liked the idea of setting up her own studio in Portland, anyway.

Didn't she?

Tears stung her eyes as she slid on her hoodie. Zachary had every right to be mad at her. She shouldn't have tried to mess with his writing career. It was his, not hers. Maybe she shouldn't have said anything since she had decided against it, but she wasn't going to regret being honest.

She picked up her phone and saw some missed calls.

Two missed calls from Zachary and a message.

Her pulse raced, pounding in her ears. Did she dare listen to it? What if he'd decided he was done with her? It was at that moment that Jasmine realized just how much he meant to her—how much she didn't want to lose him.

Shaking, she pressed the code to hear his message. She had to replay it three times before she was sure she'd heard right. He needed to apologize? And he hoped she'd hear him out?

Jasmine sat, still trembling. She didn't trust her hands to make the call. She took some deep breaths, trying to calm herself.

Would she give him the chance? Of course she would. Even though she'd convinced herself she was excited about returning to Portland, deep down, she knew that wasn't what she wanted. Not really. She could teach dance anywhere, but what really mattered was being near Zachary and seeing where their relationship would go.

If she could be with him, she'd be more than happy to keep working here at the gym if they would keep her. With as happy as they were with her, she didn't know why they wouldn't. Or she could follow some of the other Hunter brothers and find some empty retail space. That would be the best of both worlds—her own studio and being in town with Zachary.

She held up the phone to call him back, but her

hands were still unsteady and she dropped it. Even with the protective case, it bounced off the hardwood floor and skittered across the room.

Maybe it wasn't time to call him yet. She needed to pull herself together. Maybe even enough to let him know how much he'd irritated, and more importantly, hurt her.

Jasmine stood and picked up her phone, sliding it into her pocket. What she needed was a minute to clear her head. There was a park nearby, and walking around it might be exactly what she needed. It was near the other end of the building, and she wanted to avoid the blustery weather as much as she could, so she took the long way when she got out of her classroom.

As she passed the weight room, someone opened the door and she had to jump out of the way before it hit her. It took her a moment to realize it was Zachary coming out. Sweat dripped down his face, landing on his shirt in droplets.

"Zachary," she whispered.

He turned, his eyes widening. "Jasmine. Did you get my message?"

She nodded biting her lower lip.

"Will you wait for me to shower off? I really want—no, need—to talk to you. Is that okay?"

Jasmine tried not to stare at his muscles. His shirt had no sleeves, and it really showed off how well built he was. "I was just going to that park with the dragon climber."

"In this weather?" he asked.

"It doesn't bother me."

Zachary wiped sweat from his forehead before it fell into his eyes. "Okay. I'll meet you there, then. Fifteen minutes?"

"Take your time."

He nodded, and then walked down the hall toward the men's dressing room. Jasmine watched until he disappeared from sight, and then she went outside, heading for the park. The wind whipped her hair in her face, so she pulled it back into a bun like she'd had earlier. Then she pulled her hood over her head and tightened the string.

The cold air seemed to go right through the fabric. Jasmine folded her arms and tried to keep warm. It didn't help much. If she was going to stay in town and the weather didn't get any better, she'd have to invest in a coat. She probably would, anyway.

That reminded her that she hadn't called about the renter's insurance yet. It would sure be nice if they would help with some of the expenses. It would take her a while to make enough to earn enough for all she'd lost. Clothes would come first before she could get another laptop. She was just glad to have backed everything up online, even though she didn't have anything important like novels. But in some ways, she felt like her life had been on it.

She made it to the park, the wind continuing to chill her. The park was empty—what sane person would be there now? She jogged around the climbers and slides even though there wasn't a clear path. Just wood chips meeting grass. It was just a small park, but that was all she needed to clear her head. She picked up her pace until her breathing intensified.

Rain droplets sprinkled down, hitting her face. The whole thing just felt good. Jasmine had come here to think, but found it much more comforting not to. Just experiencing all there was to feel seemed to be what she needed. The wind and rain in her face, the cold chill, and the fresh air.

"Jasmine."

She turned around to see Zachary on the sidewalk. The wind blew his hair around, and he put his hand up to his forehead.

Jasmine jogged over to him.

"Do you want to go somewhere else?" he asked, squinting in the breeze.

"You don't like the park?" she asked.

"The weather."

"If you don't think you can handle it." She raised an eyebrow, challenging him.

"The wind makes it hard to talk," he said. "I owe you a meal, anyway. Why don't we find someplace to eat?"

"That way you'll have me as a captive audience?"

Her mouth had a mind of its own, but she didn't feel like bothering to rein it in.

He looked into her eyes. "I deserved both those comments."

She shrugged. "I could use something to eat, anyway."

"My car is just a block away. Want to take it? I think yours is still near my house."

"Is it?" she asked, shrugging. "I hadn't noticed."

The corners of his mouth twitched. "You haven't missed your car?"

"I've rather enjoyed the exercise, but I don't mind taking the lazy way to the restaurant."

Zachary snickered. "After the workout I've had, I'll gladly be a sloth."

"Whatever you have to tell yourself." She tried to keep from smiling, but her tone gave her away.

He took her hand, and she didn't stop him. For a moment, she thought about pulling it away, but he'd made the effort to say he wanted to apologize, and the last thing she wanted to do was to be like her parents and never forgive. They held everything over each other's heads, bringing up things they'd done ten or fifteen years earlier.

They walked to the car in silence, and Zachary held the passenger door for her. She climbed in and he closed the door. She looked around, remembering the day when they'd gone to the cemetery. Her heart softened, thinking about his vulnerability. Hopefully, that was the true Zachary Hunter, and not the one who'd gotten angry with her for trying to be honest.

He sat into the driver's side and started the car. One of the songs from Sophia's CD played.

"You really should put that online so you don't lose the playlist," she said. "Those discs are so easily damaged, and then it's just gone. Save it somewhere on a cloud."

"That's a good idea. I think I'll do that tonight." He glanced at her and smiled, appearing genuinely grateful. Then he turned back to the road and they rode in silence for the short drive. Zachary parked right outside a little barbecue place, having his choice of parking spots.

"I've never seen this place so empty," Jasmine said.

"That's how it gets when the weather turns bad. I heard the wind is here to stay, and when the cold weather comes early, it usually means we're in for an especially cold winter."

"Is it usually cold? I always thought California was warm all year."

"We get snow up here. Sometimes a lot of it. There's a big difference between the northern and southern parts of the state."

They went inside, and after they were seated and had their waters, Jasmine emptied her cup. She hadn't realized how thirsty she was. They took a few minutes to look over the menu and order their food. After the waitress took the menus, Zachary stared into Jasmine's eyes. "I can tell you're upset with me."

"Hurt is more like it."

He frowned. "Jasmine, I'm really sorry. I shouldn't have reacted like that."

She shook her head. "No, you shouldn't have."

He took a deep breath. "At first I felt like you had gone behind my back to destroy my—"

"Is this your version of an apology?" she interrupted. "It sounds like you're defending yourself."

"I'm getting there."

She wasn't convinced yet. "Go on."

He continued. "I didn't fully understand the recent changes in the publishing industry. I'd been lied to about that, and I thought you'd come this close," he held his thumb and finger a hair's width apart, "to ruining what I'd worked so hard for. I was afraid, Jasmine. I know it's not an excuse—there is none for the way I acted—but that's where I was at. The thought of losing everything really scared me."

The fear came through on his face, and Jasmine felt her heart soften again. She reached across the table and put her hand on top of his.

"You've heard of people's lives flashing before their eyes when they have a near-death experience?" he asked.

Jasmine nodded, not sure where he was going with it.

"That's what happened that afternoon. My writing career and dreams all flashed before my eyes. The thought that it could all be lost so easily shot terror through me. As wrong as it was, I took it out on you. I realize you were only trying to help, and in fact, if you had published it, you would have done more for me than my agent had in all the time I've been working with her."

She stared at him. "What are you saying?"

Zachary held her hand in both of his. "You gave me a wakeup call that I didn't know I needed. And you were right."

Twenty-Nine

~

JASMINE STARED AT HIM, TRYING to comprehend everything he'd just said.

"I'd like your help with it, Jasmine."

"You want me to help you publish it as an ebook?"

He squeezed her hand. "Yes. Let's see what happens when we do this. Together."

"Really?" she asked, trying not to show her excitement.

Zachary laughed. "Yes, Jasmine. You were right and I was wrong. Oh, so very wrong. Mostly in how I treated you."

She stared into his eyes. "It really hurt me, Zachary. The way you talked to me, and then the cold shoulder you gave me."

His face clouded over. "I wish I could take all of that back. I really do. It kills me that I hurt you. I hope you'll forgive me, but if you don't, I completely understand. And I'll accept whatever you decide." He took a deep breath. "Even if you never want to see me again."

Zachary's grip tightened around her hand.

How could she not forgive him? Jasmine squeezed back. "I do forgive you, and yes, I want to help you get it set up. I know it'll turn you into a bestselling author."

He beamed. "It means the world that you believe in me."

"What's not to believe in? You're talented, and you just need to get your work out there so the world can find it. Then word is going to spread like wildfire."

Zachary's gorgeous smile widened.

The waitress brought their food to the table and they dug in. Jasmine could see Zachary's mind at work. His face showed one expression after the next.

"You seem pretty excited," she said. "Are you really ready for this?"

"I've been ready for a long time. If the publishing houses won't have me, then we'll see what the public will do."

"From what Lana's cousin said, a lot of people the publishers wouldn't touch have done really well with ebooks."

"This could be a really good thing, actually," Zachary said. "For both readers and writers. The publishers have always controlled what gets printed, holding author's futures in their hands, and telling readers what they are and aren't going to read. It gives everyone a chance to have what they want."

"And books don't have to fit into neat, little boxes.

I've been looking around to see what's selling, and you'd be surprised. There are a lot of mixed genres. I even saw an Amish time-travel romance with vampires."

Zachary laughed. "And it was selling?"

"Yeah, it was ranked pretty well."

"Have I ever told you how lucky I am that you walked into my life?" he asked.

"I think technically, you walked into mine," she teased. "Since you walked right into me."

"That's true. And you've changed my life for the better in so many ways—in such a short period of time, too."

"I try."

Zachary laughed. They talked for a while until they finished the meal.

The waitress collected their plates. "Do you two want dessert?" she asked.

"Do you?" Zachary asked, smiling at Jasmine.

"I'll have to jog extra laps, but it'll be worth it."

They ordered ice cream sundaes.

"What am I going to do about a cover?" Zachary asked. "My agent said the publisher would take care of that. I wouldn't even have say, actually."

"Now you can have exactly what you want."

"What were you going to do when you wanted to upload it?"

"There are some sites that sell pre-designed covers. You just tell them what to put for the title and author name. I was going to use one as a placeholder until you could have one designed that you wanted."

"I can't afford that."

"Sure you can. It's only two or three hundred for an artist to create a unique cover for you."

"How much was the pre-made one?"

The desserts arrived, and Jasmine told him everything she'd learned from Erin. Zachary nodded as she spoke, obviously taking everything in. "There's so much to think about now that I'm not handing it over for someone else to take care of."

"You can do it, and I'm more than happy to help."

Zachary sighed. "I need back cover copy and maybe a proofreader. It's been edited, but I keep making changes. I've probably messed something up somewhere along the way."

"I can re-read it. And Lana wants to, also. I bet that between the two of us, we'll be able to find anything that needs fixing."

"Maybe." He took a bite of ice cream, dripping chocolate sauce onto the dish.

"So, you really want to do this?" Jasmine asked, excitement building.

He nodded. "I do. I'm sure of it."

"It'll take some work, but I bet we can get it out before too long. Do I have your permission to call Lana's cousin back?"

"Of course. Find out what you can from her. Covers, back cover copy, proofreaders, and anything I'm missing."

"And I promise not to do anything without running it by you."

He grinned. "This is going to be fun. And I couldn't ask for a better business partner."

Jasmine beamed. "Well, you might be required to help me with my business, so don't think it's a free ride."

He raised an eyebrow. "Your business?"

"I'd like to open a dance studio here in Kittle Falls."

Zachary's eyes widened and then he cleared his throat. "You want to stay here? In town? Long enough to open a business?"

She shrugged, taking the last bite of her dessert.

"How long have you been planning this?" he asked.

"I've really enjoyed teaching the girls, and the ones who have been regulars are especially delightful. They love learning and helping, and I would really miss them if I left."

"That's all?" Zachary asked, looking disappointed.

"I was thinking about opening one in Portland, but there's this guy here in Kittle Falls. I wouldn't mind sticking around to see where things go with him."

He chuckled. "Oh? Have I met him?"

"Possibly. It's a small town, and you're both locals."

"Tell him he better treat you well."

"I have a feeling he will." Jasmine tried to hold in a

smile, but couldn't.

Zachary leaned over the table. "Tell him I'll beat him up if he doesn't."

"Will do."

A phone rang.

Zachary held up his. "It's mine. Looks like they need me back in the shop. I'm glad we were able to talk this out. Are we good now?"

"I guess." She shrugged, pretending to think it over.

He made eye contact with her, and they burst out laughing.

"I'll take that as a yes." He waved the waitress over and handed her a card. She left with it and Zachary turned back to Jasmine. "Can we reschedule that date we missed the other day? I'll talk with Jake when I get to the shop."

"Sure. You want me to call Erin about the covers?"

He took her hand and helped her up. "I'd be much obliged."

The waitress returned with his card, he signed the slip, and they walked back out into the blustery cold.

"You sure you want to move here?" Zachary asked, shivering.

"I can handle the cold. I don't want to leave that guy I told you about. I think he might keep me distracted from the weather."

He wrapped his arms around her and pulled her close, kissing her. Jasmine shivered, but not from the weather. She loved being in his arms, and never wanted to leave. She kissed him back, wrapping her arms around him.

"Mmm. I could stay here all day," he said. "Unfortunately, my brothers would have my hide. Do you want me to drop you off at your car?"

"That would be wonderful." She pressed her palm against his and laced her fingers in between his. He was so much warmer than she, so she leaned against him, warming up.

"You make it hard for me to go to work," Zachary said, running his hand through her hair.

"I wouldn't want to get you in trouble." She forced herself to step back.

"Eh, they're my little brothers. I can take them."

The wind blew harder, sending a branch near them. Zachary grabbed her shoulders and moved her out of the way.

"We'd better get in the car," he said. They ran over and hurried inside, barely missing another branch.

"That's some crazy wind," Jasmine said, trying to catch her breath.

Zachary started the car. "I'm afraid summer's officially over."

They discussed the possibility of a rough winter on the short drive to the Hunter house. Zachary helped her out of his car and into hers.

"Call me later," she said.

"As soon as I can." He gave her a quick kiss on the forehead before closing her door and waving.

Jasmine drove to Lana's. Just as she was about to get out, her phone rang. She didn't recognize the number and answered it, hoping it was about the rental insurance. She needed to get that moving so she could replace her stuff.

"Hello?"

"Jasmine Blackwell?"

"Speaking."

"This is Nurse Keller from the hospital. Do you have a minute to discuss your mother's care?"

Her heart sank. "Yeah. What's going on?"

"She's agreed to rehab."

"What?" Jasmine exclaimed. "Really?"

"Yes. She wants to work past her addictions and get clean. It took some convincing, but between wanting to avoid jail and dealing with her withdrawals, she thinks she's up for it. But she's going to need some support. Do you think you can provide that? She asked specifically for you."

Jasmine took a deep breath. She didn't want to deal with her mom's problems, especially with everything going so well with Zachary. On the other hand, if her mom was serious about cleaning up, maybe they could both have a happily ever after. Maybe. She wasn't going to hold her breath.

"Are you still there?" asked the nurse.

"Yeah, sorry. As long as she's serious, I'll be her support."

"Oh, good. We're trying to find the right facility to send her to, but she won't agree to anything unless you're here."

She never thought she'd see the day her mom wanted help. "Why does she want *my* help?"

"Your mom said she's trying to get out of a bad living situation, and you're the most responsible person she knows."

That was the nicest thing her mom had ever said about her—even if the nurse had reworded it to make it sound better, as Jasmine suspected. "Um, okay. I can be there in about a half an hour."

Jasmine ended the call and pulled out of her spot, unable to believe the events of the day.

When she stepped to the hospital room, her mom sat in a chair, flipping through a magazine.

"Mom."

She looked up and half-smiled, showing her yellowed teeth. "Jas. You came."

Jasmine stepped closer. "You really want to turn your life around?" she asked, not hiding her disbelief. Jasmine had no reason to believe her mom.

"I do. That's why I came to you in the first place, but didn't have the self-control to stop. Wish it hadn't come down to this, but here I am. Sorry about your apartment."

"What about everyone else's condos?" Jasmine snapped.

"Those, too," she muttered. "I'm ready to change, and now I see my need for help."

Jasmine studied her face, waiting for the other shoe to drop.

Her mom held up the magazine in her lap. "This is the rehab place they want to send me. What do you think?" She handed it to Jasmine.

She glanced it over. "It seems okay. I don't really know much about those places, though."

"I can't focus on any of these details, so I need to know what you think. It's close to here, but I don't know if you're staying. You move around a lot, don't you?"

Jasmine hesitated. How much of her life did she dare sharing with her mom? "When I was performing, I did." Jasmine sat in the seat across from her. "I just finished school to teach dance. Well, when my internship is complete, I'll be done."

"Will you be close by if I need you?" asked her mom, her eyes widening. "I know I haven't done anything to deserve your help, Jas, but it would mean a lot." She stared into Jasmine's eyes. Her eyes were bloodshot and she had dark bands underneath.

"I plan on staying in Kittle Falls for a while—just not in the condo."

Her mom frowned and looked down, playing with

her ragged fingernails. "I'm really sorry about that."

"I know. And yeah, if you need me, I'll be around. What about Dad?"

"What about him?"

"Are you going to ask him to support you through the process, too?" Jasmine asked.

"That man is never going to change. The only way *I'll* be able to move on is to stay away from him."

Jasmine nodded. "That's probably for the best. Do you think you'll be able to? You've been with him a long time."

"I'm already happier after this little bit of space from him."

"What if you decide you want to go back to drinking? Or smoking?" asked Jasmine.

Her mom shook her head. "I want to get clean. Rehab, support groups, whatever it takes. Can you press that red button on the bed? I'm ready to have the nurses get my transfer ready. You think that place looks good?" She gestured toward the brochure.

"As best I can tell." Jasmine pressed the nurse call button. "Want me to check the ratings online?"

She rubbed her temples. "If you can."

Jasmine pulled out her phone and did a quick search. "Seems to be the best rated one around here."

"Okay." Her mom slouched in the chair.

"Anything else?" Jasmine asked.

"The light is really bright, and I'm starving."

Jasmine stood and dimmed the overhead lights. "Are they feeding you enough?"

"I'm always hungry. They say it's from giving up the cigarettes."

A nurse came in. "What can I help you with?"

"My mom's ready to get set up with the rehab unit," Jasmine said.

"Good. Let's get her set up."

Jasmine took a deep breath, hoping her mom was serious.

Thirty

~

ZACHARY SQUEEZED JASMINE'S HAND. "I think this place is perfect for your studio. It won't take much to transform it."

The empty retail space in front of them was a former karate studio, and already had much of what Jasmine needed for her dance studio, including mirrors on nearly every wall. They would need to tear out the floor mats, but there were supposed to be nice hardwoods underneath. Those would just need to be buffed.

Jasmine stepped back, letting go of his hand. "And my settlement from the fire should cover most of it. I really can't believe how much they awarded me."

He moved over to her and wrapped his arms around her from behind. Her hair brushed against his face, tickling it. "Everything has fallen into place."

Zachary's phone beeped.

"Another sale?" Jasmine asked and then laughed. "You need to turn those notifications off."

"I love that sound."

"You know, they say you shouldn't check the sales more than once a week."

"I've never been one to follow advice."

She shook her head. "Then keep it up. Turn up the volume. Shout it from the rooftops."

"Are you trying to use reverse psychology on me?"

"Who, me?"

His phone beeped again, indicating another book sale. He rolled his eyes. "Okay, okay. I'll turn them off." He pulled out his phone and silenced the notifications.

Zachary slid his hands down her arms and turned her around, gazing into her eyes. "You can try that on me as much as you want. I'm just glad that you're staying in town. You've managed to walk into my life and turn it upside-down—in the best way possible. I'd still be chasing down agents and publishers if it weren't for you."

"And who knows where I'd be?" she asked. "Back in Oregon, lonely and bored."

He kissed her nose. "We're both better off. Is your mom still doing well in rehab?"

"They're supposed to re-evaluate later this week, but it sounds promising. Last week, they told me she was their star 'student.' I had serious doubts, but in this case, I'm so glad to be wrong."

Zachary kissed her cheek. "Me, too, beautiful."

"It was so nice of your parents to offer her a place to stay until she gets on her feet."

"And I thought it was pretty nice of that random dance instructor to offer her a job doing office work, too."

Jasmine shoved him playfully. "Unfortunately, I can't imagine anyone else hiring her. She hasn't worked in over twenty-five years, and she will have just came out of rehab."

"Still, it was quite nice of you. Especially after everything you've told me about your history."

"If she's ready to turn over a new leaf, then I want to help her."

"Kind of ironic how the fire she started is helping to pay for her first job."

Jasmine shrugged. "Like you said, everything has worked out. Are you ready for the long drive? I can't wait to get this graduation over and finally be a real instructor."

Zachary stood taller, his heart jumping into his throat. Not only were they driving to Portland for her graduation, but they were going to get engaged—assuming she said yes. His heart raced, just thinking about it. He slid his hand into his pants pocket where the ring was stored safely.

"Zachary?"

"I'm ready. Are you?"

She nodded. "I hope so."

"You're going to do great. Let's go." He had to get his mind off the proposal before he talked himself out of it. She would say yes, but his nerves were making him doubt.

Lana had asked Jasmine a bunch of questions about what style of engagement rings she liked and her dream proposal. Luckily, she had always wanted a traditional one with the guy lowering onto one knee and expressing his devotion. Zachary had thought about planning out a complicated, unique proposal, but with his nerves as they were, he'd be better off with something simple.

Zachary had been worried that Jasmine would figure out why Lana was asking all the questions, but Lana swore it was typical girl talk.

Brayden had gone with Zachary to the jeweler, helping him to find the exact ring that Jasmine wanted. Then Brayden had even roll played with Zachary, pretending to be Jasmine—Zachary had been *that* nervous about the proposal. No surprise since his gift was writing, not performing.

They climbed into Zachary's car and he started it, his palms sweating. He took a deep breath again, but Jasmine didn't appear to notice his nervousness.

She pulled out her phone. "I made you a playlist of my favorite songs."

He looked over at her, surprised. "You did?"

"I hope it's okay. I don't want to encroach on Sophia's CD."

"Never. I bet she'd be glad I'm listening to something new. Maybe she can even hear this one from somewhere."

Jasmine squeezed his hand. "Maybe she's even with Carter listening."

"I'd like to think so." He pulled out of the parking spot, curious to hear the music she'd chosen. He enjoyed the first song, tapping his fingers on the steering wheel as he made his way toward the highway. They made lighthearted conversation the whole way until they came to Portland.

"Do we have time to get something to eat?" she asked.

He checked the time. "I wish. But I don't want you to be late to your own graduation."

"It's not a real graduation. I'm just—"

Zachary put his finger over her lips. "It's real, and I'm proud of you. Top of your class."

Her face turned red. "It's not a big deal. I'm just getting a certificate."

"Don't downplay it. You did great, and you deserve your day."

They climbed out of the car and Jasmine brought out her phone. "Hey. We do have time to get something to eat."

Zachary shook his head, his heart rate increasing. "Nope. You need to get there early and make sure you're prepared."

They walked toward the building and Zachary stopped in front of a pretty rose bush.

"What's the matter?" Jasmine asked.

Zachary's heart pounded against his rib cage. He was about to break into a sweat. Taking a deep breath, he bent down. "What's that?"

"What?" she asked.

Zachary kneeled on the ground, a tiny rock pressing into his knee through the pants. He dug his hand into his pocket, finding the ring. His heart pounded even faster as he pulled it out. "This." He held it out in front of her.

Jasmine gasped, covering her mouth with her hands. Her eyes widened and shone.

He took her hand and kissed it, preparing his words. "Like I said back at your studio, you've changed my life, Jasmine. The last month and a half have been the best of my life. You've supported and challenged me—given me exactly what I need. I know this probably seems crazy after such a short time, but I can't live without you. Will you marry me?"

Jasmine squealed, nodding frantically. "Yes!"

Zachary slid the ring on her finger. It was a perfect fit, thanks to Lana finding out her size for him. He stood and picked her up, spinning her in a hug.

"Would it be okay if I had this dance?"

She looked around. "You want to dance? In the parking lot?"

"I've been practicing."

"With whom?" Jasmine asked.

Heat crept into Zachary's cheeks. "Cruz."

Jasmine threw her head back and laughed. "Cruz? You danced with him?"

"Can we forget about that and just dance?"

"Did you record any of it?" she teased.

"You think this is pretty funny, don't you?"

She kissed him. "I think it's incredibly sweet you'd do that for me."

Zachary kissed her back and then pulled her close. He slid his hand down to the small of her back, and held her other hand in his. Though there was a slight breeze, the sun still shone, reflecting light from the ring.

Just as they finished the dance, a rustling noise sounded not far away.

"Did we miss it?" someone called.

They turned around. All of Zachary's brothers, his parents, Lana, Tiffany, and Kate were headed their way.

Jasmine gave him a questioning look. "Did you invite them?"

"Not really." He laughed.

The girls crowded around Jasmine, admiring the ring. The guys congratulated Zachary. Cruz held up his fist.

Zachary bumped Cruz's fist with his own. "Thanks for helping me dance. It really worked."

Cruz glanced at the other guys. "I don't know what you're talking about."

"Okay," Zachary said.

"I want to see you guys dance," Kate said.

"So do I," agreed Zachary's mom.

Zachary felt his face heat up, but as soon as Jasmine was back in his arms, he forgot about everyone else.

He led her, gliding along the concrete in a beautiful, well-choreographed dance. His heart pounded steadily against his chest as he looked into the beautiful eyes of his new fiancée.

Meet the Hunter brothers of Kittle Falls...

Seaside Surprises

Work hard. Play often. Love unconditionally.

Tiffany Saunders is on the run. When she winds up stranded in a seaside town, she wants nothing more than to forget her horrific past and kept moving. But a chance meeting with a handsome local changes everything.

Jake Hunter has some deep emotional scars and is trying to cope with running the family business. The last thing he wants is a relationship—until a mysterious brunette walks into his store and complicates it all.

Tiffany prefers to keep the painful memories of the past where they belong—in her rear view mirror. But dark secrets cannot stay hidden forever. Just as the walls around Tiffany's heart start to come down, the past catches up with her. Will true love be able to conquer all?

Seaside Heartbeats

Sometimes love shows up when you least expect it.

After years of hard work, architect Lana Summers just wants a relaxing vacation in the beach town of Kittle Falls. Instead, she suffers unexpected heart problems, and finds herself in the office of a gorgeous cardiologist—who only makes her heart work harder.

Brayden Hunter left his successful cardiology practice in Dallas to be closer to his aging parents. Focused on building a health care clinic in his hometown, he doesn't want any distractions. However, the beautiful Lana is one he can't seem to avoid.

As their attraction grows, they stumble upon a 160-year-old mystery. Brayden catches her adventurous spirit as they chase after answers, and he can't help falling for her. But can he convince her to stay in the small beach town and with him?

Seaside Kisses

People change, but some feelings last forever.

Rafael Hunter never thought he'd return to Kittle Falls, but life gave him no other choice. Los Angeles chewed him up, spit him out, and sent him back to square one.

Amara Fowler has lived in the small beach town her entire life. She's overcome her shyness to grow into the woman she always knew she could be, but she never forgot her secret crush. When the alluring Rafael returns, he can't help but stir in her a whirlwind of old feelings.

They've both changed so much. Has life kept them incompatible or has it molded them into a matching set?

Seaside Christmas

He can't stand her. She thinks he's crazy. Will their feelings stay etched in permanent ink?

Cruz Hunter has always stuck out in his small hometown. Now that he's covered in tattoos, the residents peg him as even more of an outcast. It seems like the whole world is against his dream of opening a local tattoo parlor.

When he finally finds the perfect place for his new business, Cruz discovers a pastor and his daughter have already bought it. The only thing more irritating than the change in his plan is Talia, a beautiful and feisty argument in a dress. Cruz would like nothing more than to have her out of his life and his mind, but for some reason, she's the only thing he can think about.

If Cruz and Talia can stop arguing long enough, opposites may do much more than attract.

Excerpt from Seaside Kisses
Now Available

AMARA TURNED AROUND AND LEFT the candy shop a second time. She turned to head for the main part of town where most of the restaurants were.

She stopped in her tracks.

A gorgeous, dark-haired man stepped out of a shop that had been empty retail space all summer. He wore a deep purple silk shirt that was obviously designer.

Rafael Hunter.

What was he doing in town? She hadn't seen him in at least a decade. Not even the couple times she'd heard of his brief returns. After graduation, Rafael had pretty much high-tailed it out of town, like at least half the kids in their class—and every other one before and after them.

He pulled a key out of his pants pocket and locked the store.

Could he be in town permanently? Was it possible he owned a store only a few doors down from the candy shop?

Amara stared, feeling like a fool, reminded of the girl she had been in school. Overweight, unappealing, the weight of her thick, nerdy glasses sitting on her nose as they had all those years before. It didn't matter that she'd lost the weight, that she now wore contacts. Seeing Rafael sent her right back to the painful days she'd rather forget.

She thought about saying hi, but couldn't bring her feet to move. Rafael had been the hottest boy in their class—just like all five of the Hunter brothers had been in their respective classes. There wasn't a girl in Kittle Falls who hadn't crushed on at least one of the five brothers at some point.

Rafael had been Amara's secret crush. And what made that even more difficult was that they had often been placed together in classes because alphabetically, their last names were so close. There hadn't been any kids in their class with a last name in between theirs. Amara had been too shy to talk to him, but had always admired his sense of humor and ability to find the good in any situation.

He leaned against the door he'd just locked, staring at his phone. Amara took the opportunity to study him. He was clean-shaven and even better looking than he'd been in school with his broader shoulders and rugged stubble.

Without warning, Rafael lowered his phone and looked her way. She'd been caught staring. Heat crept into her cheeks.

"Rafael!" she called, waving. If she pretended it was

no big deal, maybe she could save face.

He arched an eyebrow, not appearing to recognize her.

Amara's heart sank. After all those times sitting next to her in class, and he didn't know who she was. She forced a smile and walked over. "I don't think I've seen you since graduation." Maybe that would help to ring a bell. She smiled wider. "How are you?"

Rafael continued looking at her. It was obvious he hadn't a clue who she was.

"I heard you have a crazy successful business in LA," Amara said. "That must be so exciting. I'm running my parents candy shop with Alex." *That* had to tell him who she was. Alex had run with the same crowd of kids that Rafael had. "Actually, Alex and I own it now. My parents opened a shop near Disney Land, which is super successful. We almost never see them anymore." Ugh. Why did her mouth have to run when she was nervous? He didn't need to know all that.

Rafael's face finally registered recognition. "Four-Eye—I mean, Amara Fowler?"

Amara grimaced. "Four-Eyed Fowler. You can say it. Everyone did."

"I apologize." He stared at her. "You look completely different. I can't believe—I mean, you look great."

It took her a moment to recover. Rafael Hunter had just said she looked great? Great? "Well, I got contacts, so the old nickname doesn't really fit anymore."

Rafael shook his head. "No, it certainly doesn't."

"So, what brings you back to Kittle Falls? Looking into retail space?"

He glanced behind him. "I've got that space, and I'm close to ready to open."

"Oh, like a satellite location?"

"More like starting over." Neither his face nor his tone indicated whether that was a good or bad thing.

Amara forced another smile. "Well, that sure sounds exciting. Looks like we're going to be neighbors." She gestured toward the candy shop. "I don't want to keep you any longer, but welcome back. If you need anything, just stop in."

"Thanks. It's good to see you again, Amara."

"You, too." She spun around and walked away, trying to catch her breath. She had so many questions, but thankfully, she hadn't babbled on anymore than she had at the start of the conversation.

Amara couldn't think straight and seemed to have lost her appetite.

Author's Note

Thanks so much for reading Seaside Dances. I hope you're enjoying the series as much as I am. It was a step out of my comfort zone writing sweet romance after writing paranormal romance and contemporary suspense, but I really love the Hunters! Each one is different, and has their own endearing qualities. It was fun to write about Zachary since he's a writer, too!

Anyway, if you enjoyed this book, please consider leaving a review wherever you purchased it. Not only will your review help me to better understand what you like—so I can give you more of it!—but it will also help other readers find my work. Reviews can be short—just share your honest thoughts. That's it.

Feel free to let me know your thoughts. I'd love to hear from you. The easiest way to do that is to join my mailing list (link below) and reply to any of the emails.

Want to know when I have a new release? Sign up here (stacyclaflin.com/newsletter) for new release updates. You'll also get a free book!

I've spent many hours writing, re-writing, and editing this work. I even put together a team who helped with the editing process. As it is impossible to find every single error, if you find any, please contact me through my website and let me know. Then I can fix them for future editions.

Thank you for your support! I really appreciate it—and you guys!

Other Books by Stacy Claflin

The Transformed series

The Gone series

Mercy Books

Chasing Mercy

Searching for Mercy

Visit StacyClaflin.com for details.

CPSIA information can be obtained
at www.ICGtesting.com
Printed in the USA
LVHW03s0001200618
581338LV00001B/189/P